DEAD LOCK

B. David Warner

D0283367

Black Rose Writing
www.blackrosewriting.com

© 2011, 2012 by B. David Warner

All rights reserved. No part of this book may be reproduced, stored in a retrieval system or transmitted in any form or by any means without the prior written permission of the publishers, except by a reviewer who may quote brief passages in a review to be printed in a newspaper, magazine or journal.

The final approval for this literary material is granted by the author.

Second printing

All characters appearing in this work are fictitious. Any resemblance to real persons, living or dead, is purely coincidental.

ISBN: 978-1-61296-015-9

PUBLISHED BY BLACK ROSE WRITING

www.blackrosewriting.com

Printed in the United States of America

Dead Lock is printed in Garamond

Cover photo by Eric Treece

www.coloradostormchaser.com

Dead Lock is dedicated to my family:
my wife, Marlene, daughters Margi Warner and Andi
Hernandez, and my son-in-law John Paul Hernandez.

ACKNOWLEDGMENTS

While Dead Lock is a work of fiction, the plot is based on a fear that was very real during the early days of WWII. If the locks at Sault Ste. Marie had been destroyed, the Allied war effort would have been badly compromised.

I've attempted to keep the background as factual as possible. There actually were some 7,300 troops stationed at the Soo in late 1942 and early 1943, armed with anti-aircraft weapons. There were submarine nets and barrage balloons – balloons that sometimes broke loose from their moorings and drifted away to be found miles away.

This kind of accuracy requires a dedication to research. And for information that helped *Dead Lock* come to life I thank a number of people, beginning with Bernie Arbic. His excellent histories, **City of the Rapids** and **Upbound Downbound,** formed the base of my knowledge of the region and its past. I also thank Paul Sabourin who spent many hours showing me locations where actual events took place.

The late Chuck Payment provided extremely helpful input: he worked for the *Soo Evening News* in 1941. Dr. Donald McKinnon, once assigned to Army Intelligence, was at the dedication of the MacArthur Lock, and gave me a valuable glimpse into the happenings of that day, as well as life in the Soo at that time.

To Ralph Kiefer and Heide Borsdorf go thanks for providing the German translation in the chapter on the Enigma.

Thanks to Margaret Chaney and Jean MacLellan for their knowledge of Detroit in the 40s and what it was like to work on the *Detroit Times* newspaper.

Paul Bressler and "David" of Allexperts.com contributed a great deal of advice on fine wine of the time. Paul Sutton lent insight into the anti-aircraft weaponry used at the Soo during WWII.

Finally, thanks go to Eric Treece for his cover photo and to Chris Ivy for the photo of the author.

Prologue

On October 4, 1942, almost three years into what had by now become known as World War II, the top secret British MI6 branch at Bletchley Park decrypted a German Enigma radio transmission that referenced an attack on the locks at Sault Ste. Marie, Michigan, USA. The transmission indicated the assault would take place the following year during dedication ceremonies for the new MacArthur Lock. The attack was scheduled to wreak maximum damage on both property and the lives of the thousands of people who were expected to be present during the ceremony.

Ninety percent of the iron ore that supplied the Allied war effort passed through these locks by lake freighter, and destroying them would shut down every airplane, tank, ship and munitions plant in the United States.

The message was taken very seriously.

1

Detroit, Michigan
Wednesday, June 16, 1943
25 days before the dedication of the MacArthur Lock

The night sky had cleared over the tree-lined neighborhood of modest two story homes on Detroit's east side. The clouds responsible for the puddles on the street and the damp mist sparkling in the grass had drifted eastward and now hung somewhere over southern Ontario, Canada.

Windows were open to this warm humid evening and strains of Kay Kyser's *They'll Be Bluebirds Over the White Cliffs of Dover* played somewhere in the distance.

Hundreds of onlookers gathered behind rope barriers installed on either side of a small white house in the middle of the block. People stood side by side, some clutching folded umbrellas in case the rain should return. They waited, their attention focused on the front door of the home where nearly an hour ago a gunman had appeared demanding a ransom for the woman he held captive and giving the police sixty minutes to produce the money along with an automobile he could use to make an exit.

Inside the ropes, uniformed police and officials in street clothes milled about, some pausing to talk in small groups. Four squad cars, fastback 1942 Chevrolets, were parked side by side at the curb. With their noses facing the home they resembled huge black cats poised on their haunches, their yellow eyes casting beams of light against the front of the house, turning its white exterior into lemon icing. The fact that the headlights violated the Office of Civil Defense-ordered blackout didn't matter. Tonight was different.

A woman's life was at stake.

The gunman's eleven o'clock deadline was nearing and he would reappear in minutes, holding his hostage in front of him. He would repeat his demand for a thousand dollars cash and a car. The police had a strict policy against negotiations of this sort and would try to stall the man, whom the first officers on the scene had identified as a mob thug named Frank Valvano. It wouldn't take long for Valvano to understand he was being conned and all hell would very likely break loose.

Valvano was well known by the Detroit police force as a psychopathic killer who was tolerated by his mob bosses only because of his skill with both gun and knife and his willingness to follow orders without question. Since the events of this evening had blown up in his face, Valvano seemed to have decided that his stock with his bosses had run out. His demands for money and transportation sprung from a desire to escape both authorities and the Detroit mob.

Inside the house with the gunman was a woman named Kate Brennan. A reporter for the *Detroit Times*, she had been writing a series of front page articles exposing the mob as the perpetrators behind a rash of counterfeit gasoline ration stamps. Since early 1942 the government had instituted rationing that limited most Americans to five gallons of gasoline a week. Despite the waves of patriotism on the Home Front the bogus stamps proved widely popular. They netted eleven million dollars a year and the mob, which could always be counted upon to put money ahead of patriotism, was understandably upset by the articles. They had sent Valvano to threaten the woman at the very least, and to kill her if she insisted on continuing the crusade.

Arriving home shortly after nine o'clock, Brennan found Valvano in her living room. She had successfully avoided his grasp and run into her bedroom, where she locked the door. She was on the bedroom telephone with the police when Valvano broke down the door and smashed the phone against the wall.

But it was too late; the police were on the way.

A lone police rifleman stood on the lawn across the street from the house, his M1C sniper rifle resting against the damp trunk of a twenty-foot elm. Oblivious to both the people and the occasional drop of moisture from the leaves above him, his attention was riveted on the front door of the house. The rifleman's name was Ben Hatfield and this sort of operation was not new to him. He had been a sniper in WW1, serving in the Fourth U.S. Marine Brigade under Colonel James Harbord. He took part in the famous 1918 Battle of Belleau Wood where he killed a number of the enemy, some as far away as half a mile. Now in his late fifties, Hatfield, who rode a desk and shuffled papers downtown, had to be content with sporadic assignments such as tonight's. He kept his eye sharp at the range, never firing fewer than two hundred rounds a week. Because the war had made bullets scarce, he had to pack his own.

He had been told the woman stood five feet six inches, Valvano five feet nine. The gunman would be crouched behind his hostage, of course, and there would be precious little room for error. The kill shot would take every ounce of skill Hatfield owned. But the brass downtown were confident enough in his ability to give him the green light to shoot if he saw an opening.

Hatfield had just glanced down at his watch when the corner of his eye caught sight of movement in the doorway. His attention shifted quickly back to the M84 scope on his rifle.

The gunman was coming out.

2

As the ranking police officer on the scene, the life of the young woman rested in the hands of Captain Lyle Banner, a 24-year veteran of the Detroit force.

At the first sight of the gunman, Banner decided on a cautionary move, ordering those inside the roped area to take cover behind the police cars. Banner himself was standing, head and shoulders exposed, behind the car directly in front of the doorway where the gunman and his hostage had appeared.

The wooden door was open and the two stood behind a screen door, Valvano holding the woman in front of him. Even through the screen Banner could see she was blinking from the glare of the squad car headlights that bathed the entire scene in a shade of ocher.

Valvano shouted to the police to douse the headlights. Banner gave the order and the lights were switched off.

Approximately one hundred feet behind Banner, Hatfield watched the drama unfold through his scope. With lights from the living room illuminating her, he saw the woman clearly through the screen door. But he could barely make out the silhouette of the gunman's head and torso behind her. It was no more visible than the dark outline of a pencil sketch. To a marksman like Hatfield, the distance of a hundred feet to the target wasn't the dilemma; the problem was a distance that could be measured in mere millimeters between the gunman and his hostage.

"You got good news for me or do I kill the woman?" Valvano shouted through the screen.

"The kind of money you asked for is scarce this time of night," Banner shouted back. "We're working on it."

"You'd better work fast. You've got fifteen more minutes before I kill the woman and myself. You know I'll do it."

Banner glanced down at his watch. He had no doubt the threat was real. Valvano was wanted in three states for a score of murders and had nothing to lose.

Through his scope, Hatfield saw the hint of the man, but knew he couldn't chance a shot. In the dim light he could see that Valvano held a small pistol against the woman's temple with his right hand, his left arm wrapped around her upper torso. She was an attractive woman in her late twenties or early thirties with a thin, straight nose and large, expressive eyes.

Hatfield moved the tip of the rifle muzzle downward, peering through the scope, looking for any chance of a shot. When he saw what she was doing, he couldn't help but think, *God, that woman has balls!*

The woman's hands were pinned against her body, but it was obvious that she was trying to signal someone, anyone, with her fingers. Downward and out of Valvano's view she was pointing toward her left hand with her right index finger. With her left fist clenched, she extended each of three fingers, one at a time, in a one-two-three counting motion.

God, that woman has balls.

Hatfield moved the scope back to the woman's face. She had every right to be terrified, most people would be. But instead of fear her eyes burned with defiance. If she could make someone understand, she was going to hit the ground on the count of three.

"Captain!" Hatfield fought to get Banner's attention. The captain was busy calling back and forth to the gunman on the porch, still trying to stall, to negotiate. Something. Anything.

"Captain Banner!" Banner finally swung around.

"Captain, have one of your men shine a spotlight on me. I want the two inside the house to see me."

Banner hesitated, then looked at his watch. Three minutes had already gone by since Valvano's threat to kill the woman and himself.

"Captain. Please. It's important."

Banner gave the order and a police sergeant swung the spotlight from one of the cars backwards to illuminate Hatfield behind the tree. At the sight of the sniper, Valvano seemed to pull the woman even closer, his pistol pressed to her temple.

"Your sniper doesn't scare me," Valvano called out. "He misses and she's dead. His bullet or mine."

Hatfield had to be sure the woman knew he understood her signal. Holding the M1 against the tree trunk, he raised and lowered the barrel slowly three times.

Then he called: "Okay, lights out."

3

Back in the scope, Hatfield watched the woman's eyes and saw by the way she looked straight at him that she had understood. He lowered the scope to look at her hands . . . but they weren't moving.

What the hell was she waiting for?

Raising the scope again, he saw. The gunman had tightened his grip around the woman's head and neck; there was no way for her to get loose enough to drop.

Now her lips were moving. She said something, perhaps asking him to loosen his hold, because that's what he seemed to do as she let out a breath. Her eyes dropped to her hands once again. Hatfield lowered his scope. She was ready.

One. Her left index finger shot out.

Two. The middle finger came out and Hatfield raised the scope of his rifle back up to head level. He knew there would be just one chance.

One shot.

With the woman's face now filling his scope, Hatfield couldn't see her finger signals. But on what surely would have been the count of three her head dropped from the frame, exposing the silhouette of Valvano's face for an instant before he moved to raise her up.

Not quickly enough.

Traveling at 2,837 feet per second, the M1's .30-06 slug tore through the screen and the right side of Valvano's scalp. His head disappearing in a cloud of red mist as his body slammed backward into the room. Regaining her balance the woman stood with her back to the screen door, glaring down at her would-be-killer and shaking her fist.

God, that woman has balls.

4

If you're wondering where the woman on the porch got the guts to act so bravely, I don't blame you.

I lay in bed later that evening wondering the same thing.

I rolled over and reached into the drawer of my bed stand and retrieved an envelope with its carefully folded paper inside. I read the printed message for what must have been the one-thousandth time:

> *Mr. and Mrs. Ronald Strickland request your presence*
>
> *at the wedding of their son Ronald Jr. to*
>
> *Kate Brennan,*
>
> *daughter of the late Harold "Buck" and Margaret Brennan.*

Ronny and I had picked the perfect date for our wedding: Valentine's Day fell on a Saturday in 1942. But it never happened. World War II got in the way.

Ron enlisted in the Navy the day after Pearl Harbor, a cloudy, snowy Monday in December. He got to stay home for Christmas, a time I'll remember forever, because it was our last together. Ron shipped out for the Great Lakes Naval Station on January 2, 1942, a cold, dark day. But not as dark as June 5, when word came that Ronny had been killed at Midway. Three Japanese Val dive bombers had penetrated the defenses of the *Yorktown*. Shells hit the first plane and it spun out of control. But not before it released a bomb that hit the carrier on the starboard side, blasting a 10-foot wide hole in the flight deck and killing Ronny and his shipmates who were manning the two anti-aircraft guns nearby.

The Battle of Midway was hailed as a great U.S. victory. The Japs lost four of their fleet carriers; but I lost Ronny. I cried every day for weeks. There's still an emptiness that surfaces when I pass one of the places we frequented, or hear a joke I know would have made Ronny laugh.

The healing process went much too slowly. In time, I got past Ronny's death, but I know I'll never get over it. The emotional wound, worse by far than any physical blow I'd ever suffered, left me with a scar that brought a new outlook on life. Things that once seemed terribly important aren't quite so vital. Events that once would have terrified me aren't so frightening.

I think that's what saved my life tonight.

5

The next morning

The war in Europe and North Africa was progressing fairly well, and we were taking it to the Krauts. The front page of the *Detroit Times* would report later today that nearly 700 RAF and RCAF bombers had reached the Ruhr steel center at Muelheim for the first time since 1940.

But here in the U.S.A., I found myself embroiled in a war of my own.

"Get lost Kate."

Wells Mayburn, *Detroit Times* Managing Editor, took a deep drag from the Pall Mall in his meaty fingers and blew a stream of white smoke into the air. "I mean it; you've got to get out of the city. Hide out for a couple weeks."

It was eleven hours since I'd come within a gunman's heartbeat of taking a bullet in my brain and my boss Wells Mayburn was laying it on the line. Police Inspector Charles McKinley and I were in Wells' cluttered, smoke-filled office at the *Detroit Times* Building. We had gathered around Mayburn's conference table, but no one sat.

I took a pull from the Chesterfield I held in my hand. I'd quit smoking a couple of years after college, but started again after Ron was killed.

"I can't leave now, Wells," I said. "I'm days from cracking this counterfeiting ring wide open."

Okay, so I exaggerated. I'd been writing a series of front-page stories covering a ring of gasoline ration stamp counterfeiters. With the war on gasoline was sold practically a teaspoon at a time and stamps were gold. I hadn't busted the ring yet, but I felt close.

Mayburn knew that convincing me to leave town would be a tough sell. He took another drag and ran a thick hand through thinning black hair. "I know you're hot on their trail, Kate. Problem is: so do they."

"Look, Miss Brennan..." Inspector McKinley stepped up for a turn at bat. At an even six feet, he stood a few inches taller than me, and sported a full head of snowy white hair. "There are more Valvanos out there. You may not be lucky next time."

"Lucky, huh?" My eyes burned with a combination of anger and cigarette smoke. "You think it was luck that I kicked that bastard in the crotch when he surprised me inside my house? That I ducked to give your sniper a clear shot at his head? Why, if it weren't for me your cops would still be standing around in front of my house picking their noses."

The Inspector shot a look at Mayburn, who simply shrugged his shoulders. My attitude didn't surprise the man who'd been my editor for nearly three years.

The Inspector leaned forward, hands tightly gripping the wooden back of a chair, eyes squinting at me across the table. "I don't deny your bravery last night, Miss Brennan. But next time there might not be a chance to be brave. Their hired killer might just shoot from across the street, or come up behind you. You don't have eyes in the back of your head, do you?"

I stared him down. Realizing I wasn't going to budge, the Inspector went on. "Why don't you just tell us what you know and let us handle this?"

Mayburn winced, anticipating my response.

"My information," I said through tightly pursed lips, "is from sources who won't talk to you. I got it because they trusted me. Trusted I wouldn't turn them in or turn their names over to you. I'm not selling them out because some punk held a gun to my head. And I'm sure as hell not running away."

The Inspector threw his hands in the air, looking toward Mayburn. "You reason with her. I'm done. And I won't spend one damned cent of taxpayer money guarding a woman who's too stubborn, or too stupid to stay out of harm's way. She walks out of here, she'll be in the morgue in two days."

He had finally worn Wells down. "Kate, I'm taking you off the assignment."

I turned, ready to give him both barrels, but he held up a hand. "Temporarily," he said. "Your life is more important than any newspaper story. Go away for a few weeks; hide out somewhere. Give the Inspector time to work on the information you've published so far...and anything else you can give him without divulging your sources."

"And after that?"

"You come back. We see what the situation is and we talk about continuing the series."

I looked back and forth from Mayburn to Inspector McKinley. "What happens if the police get lucky? What if they crack the ring while I'm out of town?"

McKinley started to open his mouth, but Wells spoke first. "Inspector McKinley, if your people make arrests based on information Miss Brennan gives you, will you guarantee her first access to your arresting officers and any facts they can provide?"

McKinley's face still glowed red. "I won't guarantee any such thing."

Wells decided on a detour. "Inspector, how long has this ring been counterfeiting gasoline stamps?"

McKinley cleared his throat. "They've been active for nine months. . . more or less."

"And outside of the information published in Miss Brennan's stories in the Detroit Times, are you any closer to proving who's behind this counterfeiting than you were nine months ago?"

The Police Inspector did a slow burn as Wells went on. "If Miss Brennan helps you crack a case you've been working on for that long, doesn't she deserve some consideration?"

The Inspector let out a deep breath. "All right, all right. But she'd better give us some damn good information, or it's no deal."

I held the Inspector's eye for a long moment before speaking. "You'll get great information, Inspector. Just make damn sure your people don't screw it up."

6

It's hard as hell to say you're wrong when you know you're right. But I swallowed hard and bowed to Wells Mayburn's request that I leave Detroit.

I could have stayed in spite of Wells, tracking down the leaders of the counterfeiting ring and blowing the lid off with a series of articles unmasking the bastards. I'd like to have seen Wells refuse to publish them. Why, they would have beaten the hell out of the war news on page one; that is unless we had another Midway -- or God help us -- another Pearl Harbor.

Much as I hated to admit it, a little time off might do me some good. I had been working the counterfeiting story for a solid nine months, trailing bad rationing stamps from the gasoline stations that accepted them to the printers who turned them out. I even got a few printing operations shut down. But the really bad guys, the ringleaders, just moved on to another press.

Maybe I'd gotten stale; I'd certainly gotten careless. Forgetting to lock the door had let that punk Valvano sneak into my house. It turned out to be a close call, closer than I wanted to admit to Mayburn or McKinley.

Picking a location for my self-imposed "time out" presented no problem. My bank account wouldn't support me for long but my uncle could. G. P. Brennan owned the *Soo Morning News* in Sault Ste. Marie, Michigan, the town people simply called the "Soo". I'd spent my senior year of high school in the Soo and G.P. had promised me a job if I ever decided to move back. But I always felt too attracted to Detroit to return to Sault Ste. Marie for more than a week or two each summer. I'd miss the noisy factories and the quiet afternoons on Belle Isle. I'd miss Hamtramck and its Polish restaurants with their pierogies and kielbasa. I'd miss the nightlife of

Greektown; and Black Bottom, the center of Detroit's Negro community, with its special blend of soul food and hot jazz. As much as anything, I'd miss those marvelous Sunday mornings pouring through fresh fruits and vegetables at Eastern Market after church.

But the time had come to leave, at least for now. After the meeting in Wells' office I went home, loaded a couple of suitcases and my German Shepherd Mick into my thirty-seven Ford and hit the road.

7

Thanks to President Roosevelt's thirty-five mile-per-hour speed limit, it took two days just to get to the northern part of Michigan's Lower Peninsula. (I admit I had the speedometer close to fifty-five or sixty between towns.)

Fortunately, Wells had come up with some extra gasoline ration stamps from the *Times'* supply.

Mick and I spent our second night on the road just below the Straits of Mackinac. I rented a small cabin, one of a group huddled together with a tiny lake out back and a patch of gravel they called a parking lot in front. The bed felt comfortable though and the shower steamed good and hot in the morning.

Shortly after eight a.m., I stood on a pier at the tip of the Michigan mitten, peering out four miles across the Straits to the Upper Peninsula, waiting for the car ferry to come and transport me, Mick and my Ford to the far side. I had left my car parked in the middle of a grid of a hundred or so others, poised and waiting to drive onto the deck of the ferry.

A strong wind blew from the north, slapping cold against my face and raising white caps on the water in front of me. Waves lapped against the foundation of the pier and billowing white clouds slipped across a bright blue sky, their dark shadows racing over the waves. I took a deep breath and filled my lungs with air so clean you'd swear it came straight from the breath of God Herself.

The car ferry had just left St. Ignace on the far shore and appeared as a white dot out on the water, so I had plenty of time for a phone call to my uncle. I headed for the big gray terminal. I found the public telephone on the wall and pumped in twenty cents after giving the operator the number of the *Soo Morning News*. I made the call station-to-station; my uncle would be at his desk in spite of the early hour. He hadn't missed a day of work since my Aunt Susan died twelve years ago.

As I listened to the phone ring at the other end of the line, snapshots of my uncle developed inside my head. Standing an inch or so taller than me, he had flashing blue eyes, a thin straight nose and much more hair than most men in their mid-sixties. It was pure white and combed straight back. He looked younger than his age, due to good genes and an active lifestyle that included plenty of trout fishing and ten-hour days at the paper.

Those mental photographs wound further back in time and I pictured him holding me up to pick apples from the tree in his backyard, and standing behind me at his old gas stove as we popped popcorn.

In another mental image he sat at a desk, editing a story I had written the year I worked at the *Morning News*. It was the year I had moved – unexpectedly I might add - to Sault Ste. Marie for my senior year in high school.

I had grown up in Detroit and as a young girl I led a life most young boys dream of. I literally grew up with the Detroit Tigers.

My father was sports editor and columnist for the Detroit Free Press. Maybe you've heard of him: Harold "Buck" Brennan? During home stands at Navin Field our house served as a second home for the likes of Harry Heilmann, Topper Rigney and even the legendary Georgia Peach, Ty Cobb.

As you might imagine, my house was also very popular with the kids in school. Boys would just "happen" to drop by whenever they saw a strange car in the driveway on the chance it might belong to a Detroit Tiger.

When the team went on the road, Dad went with them, logging more rail miles than Casey Jones. That became a sore point between him and his second wife Rose until she threatened to leave him and move back to Denver, where her parents lived.

Dad refused to take her seriously until one day at the start of the Tigers' swing to the east coast, Rose put me on a train to Sault Ste. Marie and took one herself, west to Colorado.

Just after filing for divorce.

She had called my uncle, of course, to make sure I had a place to stay in the Soo. G.P. was familiar with the strains a newspaper career could put on a marriage, his own having survived nearly forty years before my Aunt Susan passed away.

After my senior year of high school, I accepted a journalism scholarship to Columbia University. Dad would visit whenever the Tigers played the Yankees, but sadly he died during my junior year of college. That left me an orphan; my real mother had been killed in a car accident when I was barely three years old.

A voice on the phone jarred me back to the present.

8

"Soo Morning News." The woman sounded very business-like.

"G. P. Brennan, please."

"One moment."

Another wait. I watched two small boys play catch on the far side of the huge waiting room. They dressed alike in red shorts, white shirts and blue caps, a reflection of the patriotism that had swept the country after that shocking December day nearly two years ago. I couldn't help hoping this damn war would be over before they and other kids like them would be called to serve in some foxhole on the other side of the world. The soldiers doing the fighting and dying now had tossed baseballs just a few years ago.

"Brennan."

"G. P., it's Kate." I had called him G. P. instead of "Uncle George" since childhood. "G. P." was his nickname, and much easier for a three-year-old to say.

"Kate! It's grand to hear from you. Say, you sound like you're next door." His voice sounded full of the warmth I remembered so well.

"I am, practically. I'm in Mackinaw City."

"Mackinaw? Why, what in blazes are you doing there?"

"Coming to visit you."

There came a pause at the other end, then, "Oh?" Strange. My beloved Uncle George didn't sound overjoyed to hear I had come to see him.

"What's wrong, G. P.? You always said I had a job with your paper anytime I wanted it."

Another pause. "It's not the job, Kate; it's finding you a place to stay."

"How about where I always stay...the upper flat in your house?"

"Why, it's rented out. Jack Crawford, my new managing editor, is living there until his house is built."

"I'll find a room somewhere in town."

"Impossible. There are no rooms. The War Department has stationed seven thousand troops here to guard the locks. Soldiers are everywhere. Fort Brady can't house them all and people are renting out their basements and garages."

I felt as though one of those huge rolling white caps out in the Straits had knocked me over. I knew the strategic importance of the Soo Locks, but I hadn't counted on this.

The iron ore from Michigan's Upper Peninsula and Minnesota's Mesabi Range was critically vital to the Allied war plants. Every lake freighter carrying ore to the steel mills in Michigan, Ohio and Pennsylvania passed through one of four locks in the St. Marys River. If anything happened to those locks, every factory in America making tanks, munitions or anything else vital to the war effort, would shut down.

"Kate..." G. P.'s voice came from somewhere in the distance. "Kate, are you there?"

"I'm here. G. P."

"Take my advice and turn around for home. The Soo is no place for you right now."

"Neither is Detroit, I'm afraid." Blow by blow I recounted my latest experience. I started with the articles on the gas ration stamp counterfeiters and the punk holding the gun to my head in the doorway of my home, and ended with Wells Mayburn's polite request to get the hell out of town.

"So you see, G. P.," I concluded, "I don't have much choice."

This time the pause stretched so long I thought the line had gone dead. A deep sigh from G.P. finally broke the silence. "Oh, all right. Come ahead. I'll find something for you."

As I hung the phone back on the hook and walked to my car I saw the ferry approaching the pier. The wind blew stronger now and the clouds had turned black. But they weren't the only darkness on the horizon. All the way across the strait I couldn't help thinking that a lack of space wasn't the real reason my uncle didn't want me in Sault Sainte Marie.

9

Sault Ste. Marie, Michigan lies at the source of the St. Marys River, where waters from Lake Superior flow through Whitefish Bay and then into the River on their journey to the lower Great Lakes. Sault Ste. Marie, Ontario, the American Soo's sister city, is just across the water. People traveling from one town to the other use a car ferry to negotiate the river.

There, between the two towns, the water level of the St. Marys drops 21 feet, creating a once insurmountable barrier for shipping. The first lock, built in the middle of the nineteenth century changed all that.

Hours after driving off the ferry, I crested a hill on Highway 2 and started down into the St. Marys River Basin and Sault Ste. Marie. Founded by French missionaries in 1668, the "Soo" is Michigan's oldest city, and the country's third oldest town west of the Appalachian Mountains.

The sun had poked out again and the scene below reminded me of Detroit's annual J. L. Hudson Thanksgiving Day Parade. There were a myriad of giant gray balloons floating a thousand feet or so above the town. The closer I got, the larger the balloons became. Like those in the Detroit department store's holiday parade, they were some thirty feet long; but instead of bright fairy tale figures, they appeared drab in color and oval in form, like dirigibles.

We drove into town, car windows down, Mick with his head stuck out in the wind, taking in the sights.

On a day when the stifling heat forces you to drive with the windows down, it's hard to imagine these streets bordered on either side by snow drifts ten feet high. But U.P. weather is Dr. Jekyll and Mr. Hyde. Each November Mr. Hyde comes riding in over Whitefish Bay on dark, black-bottomed clouds that drop flakes of snow the size of quarters. The quarters pile up on streets and sidewalks and make travel by foot or automobile not only difficult, but treacherous. There's so much snow that there is no place to put it and merchants pay men with carts to haul it away and dump piles of white slush beyond the city limits.

But today it was difficult to fathom anyone making a living hauling snow.

I drove down Ashmun Street and through Sault Ste. Marie, barely noticing the shops, restaurants and taverns. My focus remained on the balloons ahead. I had to lean forward and look straight up to see them at the very top of my windshield.

As her car slid through town, Kate Brennan couldn't have noticed Claus Krueger as she passed where he stood on the sidewalk outside Cowan's Department Store. He, too, found the giant balloons interesting, but for a far different reason.

Born in Germany, Claus Krueger had admired the United States even as a young boy. Shortly after he began to talk in his native tongue, his father had coached him in speaking Americanized English. The family planned to move to America and his father wanted him to fit in immediately. But his father's death when Claus was twelve changed those plans. That was 1924, and like many Germans, young Claus was drawn to the charismatic personality of the man known as Adolph Hitler. Hitler had been sentenced to five years in the Landsberg Prison earlier in the year, but was pardoned and released after serving only nine months.

Claus could still feel the excitement of the rallies that marked the beginning of the Nazification of Germany. The patriotic songs continued to echo in his mind, and when the United States declared war on his native land on December 8, 1941, he vowed to do whatever was asked of him to serve the Third Reich.

He joined the German Army where his intellect and his aptitude for weapons and hand-to-hand combat impressed his superiors. They were even more impressed by his command of American English. As a result, he drew what many of his countrymen considered one of the most important assignments of the war.

He was in Sault Ste. Marie to see America's precious Soo Locks destroyed and its military manufacturing brought to a dead halt.

10

I turned left onto Portage Avenue, and found myself almost directly under a group of those gigantic balloons. They were tethered on what appeared to be steel wires anchored around the four locks. The area looked dramatically different from the way I remembered it just two years or so ago. I pulled to the side of the road and took in the sight.

As teenagers, we'd swim in the south canal just above the old Weitzel Lock. A couple of the boys rigged a plank off the deck of a barge moored there, and we used it as a diving board.

You could walk up close to the locks in those days. A huge southbound freighter fresh from Lake Superior would sail into the tight space, with feet to spare on either side. The gate behind the freighter would close and water would rush out of the lock, lowering the boat twenty-one feet to the level of the waters of the St. Marys River. Then the gate at the opposite end would open and the huge boat would resume its journey south, carrying iron ore to Detroit, Cleveland or Pittsburgh.

The War had changed the locks as it had affected everything else in America. It had made the cargo of the freighters that passed through them even more precious. A tall metal fence now ringed the perimeter of the grassy park between the street and the locks themselves. Civilian guards stood outside the fence, while MPs walked the grounds inside. From the road, the four locks looked like long, narrow cement swimming pools with giant wooden gates at either end. A dozen or so of the huge balloons I noticed when I first entered town floated above.

I got out of my car and walked to the fence, pressing my face against it. A hundred feet in front of me I could see men and equipment at work on the new lock that would replace the old Weitzel. It was to be named after our famous General, Douglas MacArthur. The Poe, Davis and Sabin Locks lay on the far side of it. Plans called for the MacArthur Lock to be eight hundred feet long, large enough to accommodate the new breed of giant lake freighters. The other locks had taken years to finish; the Army Corps of Engineers vowed that the MacArthur would be completed in just 14 months. Its dedication was scheduled for July 11, and its presence, along with those huge tethered dirigibles, changed the landscape significantly.

"Barrage balloons."

I turned at the sound of the voice to find a man of thirty or so standing behind me.

11

He stood a few inches over six feet and had blond hair and sky blue eyes. He was dressed in a plaid shirt and blue jeans and had the shoulders of a lumberjack.

I must have jumped because he smiled and said, "Sorry; didn't mean to startle you. I saw you staring at those balloons and thought you might be wondering about them."

"Actually you're right," I said, sticking out my hand. "My name is Kate Brennan." A lot of men consider it too forward for a woman to offer her hand, but frankly that doesn't bother me. And it didn't seem to faze him either.

"Scotty Banyon," he said, grasping my hand. "Those barrage balloons are there to make it tough for any German planes to dive bomb the locks."

"German planes? The Krauts don't have planes capable of flying here from Germany."

"They might not have to. The fear is that they could set up a base somewhere in northern Canada, say Hudson Bay. With miles of wilderness up there, the Germans could bring in planes part-by-part by submarine and assemble them at some remote base where only the moose and caribou would see. Then fly down here and dive bomb the locks."

"The government is taking it that seriously?"

"Seriously enough to erect this fence and bring up thousands of troops.

"Say, would you like a tour?" He reached into a back pocket and brought out his wallet. "I've got a pass that'll get us inside the gate."

"Maybe some other time," I said. Four years or so ago I might have fallen for those sky blue eyes of his; but four years ago I hadn't met Ronny, and wouldn't have been through the devastating loss of someone dearer than life itself. Times like this reminded me how much I missed my fiancé and how much of the hurt remained.

I said goodbye to Scotty Banyon and set off to find out why my uncle had changed his mind about my coming to Sault Ste. Marie.

12

Walk through the front door of the *Soo Morning News*, climb six steps, cross a short hallway and you're in the long, narrow, desk-filled space known simply as the newsroom. That's where the action takes place at every newspaper and I found myself standing right in the middle of more action than I bargained for.

There were a dozen or so people involved in a flurry of motion. Those that I assumed to be reporters or editors sat typing madly. Two copyboys ran from desk to desk, grabbing sheets of paper as they came out of the reporters' typewriters. From experience I knew the deadline for tomorrow morning's edition had to be closing fast – it was time for a final edit before sending copy to the composing room where it was readied for the actual printing of the newspaper.

Some twenty feet from the group sat a young man who couldn't have been more than twenty. Red-haired and rather slight of build, he occupied a wooden desk as he watched the scene building between the two men through a pair of half-inch thick spectacles.

I maneuvered around the group and approached the young man at his desk. "What's going on over there?" I asked.

"Just the usual." He glanced up at me, then back at the small group. "It's deadline time; everyone's anxious to file a story."

I turned back to the young man. "By the way," I said, "my name is Kate Brennan."

"I know. Your uncle told everyone you were coming." He held out his right hand. "I'm Andy Checkle, but you'll probably call me Chuckles. Everyone does. That is, except for Mr. Brennan."

"What does he call you?" I asked, shaking the offered hand.

"He calls me by my last name, Checkle."

"What do you prefer?"

"Andy. Or Andrew."

"Andy it is, then."

Suddenly one of the men that had been typing fervently at his desk turned in our direction.

"Hey, Chuckles," he called, "come over here."

"Coming."

As the young man left I glanced around the large, rather long room. Toward the rear I saw a door marked "G.P. Brennan" and started toward it.

13

No one seemed to notice me heading toward the office; they were all too focused on what they were doing. I paused at the door, knocked, and waited for a response.

When none came, I knocked again. Still nothing.

I opened the door and stepped into my uncle's empty office. As I stood there, taking it all in, I could picture him seated behind his desk, pecking away with two index fingers even after fifty-some years in the newspaper business. His snow-white hair was complemented by a ruddy complexion gained through seventy years of outdoor living through zero degree winters and eighty degree summers.

I walked around his desk, past the American flag on its pole and a coat rack that held a blue suit coat, to the back wall covered with photographs. A few square feet of space captured a lifetime in black and white. Here were photos of G.P. at work and play. Some showed him with politicians, newspaper people, sports figures and a host of celebrities like Jack Benny and Walter Winchell. One with F.D.R. and *Cleveland News Courier* publisher William Peterson recorded G.P.'s selection as "Small Town Newspaperman of the Year" by the Washington Press Club.

In other photos he stood with a variety of fishing cronies and their trout – mostly brook, rainbows and steelhead. If my uncle had his choice, he'd spend every waking hour wading thigh deep in one of the Upper Peninsula's myriad trout streams.

A huge rainbow trout was mounted on a plaque that hung above the photographs. G.P. had caught it years ago on the Two Hearted River made famous in Ernest Hemingway's Nick Adams stories.

I heard muffled voices coming from a doorway to my left, probably another office. I approached the doorway and knocked. Again there was no response. I opened it a crack and could hear G.P.'s voice clearly.

"Why, if the Brits are right it means thousands of lives could be at risk," he was saying. There was a pause, and then, "How reliable do you think their information is?"

I didn't recognize the next voice, but I could hear it clearly. "The report came straight from British intelligence ... MI6."

"Those Kraut bastards! An attack on our locks during the dedication ceremony will do a lot more than destroy property. They're purposely aiming to kill thousands of innocent men, women and children."

14

My first inclination was to close the door and sneak back out to the newsroom. But before I could budge, the door flew open and my uncle stood in front of me.

"Kate. Good god, what are you doing here?"

"Sorry, G.P., I didn't mean to eavesdrop; I just came into your office looking for you and heard voices coming through this door."

I found myself looking into an office adjacent to my uncle's. I had seldom seen him look so serious.

"I suppose you caught the gist of what we were saying," G.P. said.

"I couldn't help it," I said, stepping into the office. "Do you really think there will be an attack on the locks?"

"The information you overheard is top secret, Miss Brennan," said the tall dark-haired man standing next to my uncle.

"This is Jack Crawford, Kate. He's our managing editor, the man you'll be working directly for."

"Hello, Miss Brennan. Your uncle said you were coming."

Crawford stood a few inches taller than my uncle and was heavier, with broad shoulders that tapered into a narrow waist. Like my uncle, his tie was loosened and the sleeves of his white dress shirt were rolled up.

I would have extended my hand in greeting but the tension in the room was such that I merely nodded.

G.P. looked uncomfortable. "Kate, this can't get out."

"But you said it, G.P. What about the people who are going to be there for the dedication of the new lock?"

"The Army will provide plenty of protection for them," G.P. said. "There's anti-aircraft artillery everywhere, Kate. And the heavy cables attached to those barrage balloons will cut a dive bomber to pieces."

The prospect of an attack still bothered me. "The Germans aren't foolish," I said. "If they're planning an assault on the locks, they obviously have some degree of confidence it can succeed."

This time Crawford spoke. "The artillery around the locks isn't the only reason to feel confident," he said. "There's also a very real possibility that we can stop them before they ever take off. Both our military and Canada's are combing the north provinces. They're on the lookout for any kind of clearing that might serve as an airfield for the Germans to use."

"Suppose they don't find anything?"

"The dedication ceremony won't take place until July 11th," G.P. said. "That's more than enough time to reschedule. If we have to."

"How did you find out about this raid?" I asked. Both men stood silent; then G.P. spoke.

"Why, my Washington contacts," he said. "They picked it up from the British."

"And you believe it's reliable?"

G.P. waved a hand in the air. "Yes, yes, I'm certain. Jack and I have been through all that. The information came straight from MI6. They're not admitting anything of course, but my guess is they've broken the German code."

"Why do the Germans want to kill civilians?" I asked. "What do they stand to gain?"

"Just destroying the locks would be bad enough," G.P. said. "Cutting off the supply of iron ore that goes through those locks would put our plants out of business; paralyze our entire war production. But doing it with that kind of violence would gain them another advantage. When Jimmy Doolittle and his boys bombed Tokyo last year, the physical damage was slight, but the psychological effect was catastrophic. It scared the hell out of the Japanese people knowing we could penetrate their borders."

Crawford nodded. "So far the war's been waged overseas in Europe and the Pacific," he said. "An attack inside our borders would drive a big hole in the confidence of the American people."

There was a knock at the door that led to the newsroom and G.P. held up his hand for silence.

15

It turned out to be one of the newspaper's secretaries with word that G.P. had a telephone call. He disappeared through the door to his office, leaving me alone with Jack Crawford.

Crawford broke what could have been an awkward silence.

"Glad to have you with us, Miss Brennan. It's difficult to find help during the war. Most qualified people are overseas, or stationed at some military base here."

This time I did extend my hand and Crawford took it casually. I was surprised by how large his hand was, and how rough and calloused his palm felt. More like a lumberjack or construction worker than a newspaperman.

"My uncle has always acted as managing editor of the Morning News," I said. "Frankly, I'm surprised he's entrusted the job to someone else."

"Your uncle is still very much in charge," Crawford said. But I think he wants a little more free time to himself. I came on board this January."

"I'm looking forward to being here," I said. "It's just that I'd assumed I'd be working directly with my uncle."

"No, you'll be working for me," Crawford said. "I hope that won't be a problem."

He didn't wait for an answer. "You can start Monday morning. I've already assigned the crew that'll be working this week's Saturday and Sunday editions."

Before I had a chance to say a word, G.P. came back into the room.

"That was Shirley Benoit on the phone, Kate," he said. "She was returning my call to say she's got room at her place for you to stay."

"Shirley?"

"Bought the Martin's place last January. Says she's looking forward to seeing you again."

That was great news. Shirley and I had been best friends during the year I spent here in the Soo during my parent's divorce. After school we had both moved away from the Soo. It would be wonderful to see her after all these years. But I thought about Mick, waiting patiently in the car. "Does she have room for a dog?"

"Why don't you ask her yourself? She waits tables over at Blades Larue's restaurant. I told her you'd meet her there."

"Thanks, G.P.," I said, starting for the door.

"Oh, Kate . . ." I turned back at the sound of my uncle's voice.

"I've told Mrs. Miller you'll be joining us for supper tonight. Cocktails at 6:30."

16

Blades LaRue's Restaurant and Tavern had always reminded me of a large knotty pine paneled basement with wall-to-wall tables.

An opening at the far end of the bar led to the kitchen located just behind it, and a hallway on the other side of the room provided access to the two restrooms and stairway to the large banquet facility on the second floor.

One wall of the restaurant sported a row of the mounted heads of deer, moose, elk, mountain goats and assorted other critters that had been unlucky enough to wander into the cross hairs of Blades' scope. A two-ounce slug traveling at fifteen hundred feet a second had made Blades' day and brought theirs to an abrupt end.

Black and white photos of Blades and his NHL contemporaries in action on the ice covered the area behind the bar. The town's favorite restaurant owner earned his colorful nickname playing hockey for the Detroit Red Wings. When he retired from hockey after the Wings won the Stanley Cup in 1936, the hometown boy made the locals even prouder by moving back to Sault Ste. Marie. He opened a restaurant/tavern that soon became as popular as the favorite son himself.

Today seemed no exception. Close to suppertime, the place had filled with singles and families. I noticed Shirley Benoit carrying a tray to a group of people toward the back of the room, and I grabbed the last two-top in her section.

In high school, Shirley and I were known affectionately as "the Bobsie Twins," and I had to admit we still looked a lot alike. We're both about the same height, with light brown hair and blue eyes. I also noticed with no small amount of pride that we had both stayed pretty close to our high school weights, although truthfully Shirley was always slightly bustier than me.

Slightly.

"I'll be right with you, ma'am," Shirley said breezing past my table. She'd traveled about four feet when she stopped dead in her tracks and spun around.

"Kate Brennan! I'll be damned." Good old Shirley, her vocabulary hadn't changed either. I stood up and we hugged like long-lost sisters, which we were, sort of. It was a tribute to our friendship that we still felt close, despite not having seen each other since we both moved away.

"Your uncle said you were coming. You're staying with me. I've got an extra bedroom."

I thought of my dog. "What about Mick?"

Shirley paused only a moment. "He's welcome, too."

"We don't need much room. He sleeps with me."

"Listen, honey," Shirley patted me on the arm, "your personal life is none of my business. Any friend of yours is welcome in my house." A few moments passed before I could stop laughing long enough to explain that Mick was my dog, after which Shirley had a conniption, which started me up again. Nothing had changed; it was just like the old days.

We finally settled down. "Kate, I've got to get to work or Blades'll fire me. You planning to eat here?"

"No, not tonight. G.P. invited me for supper at his house. I just dropped by to say hi."

Shirley pulled her white apron to one side and reached into the pocket of her skirt. "Here's the key to my back door, let yourself in. I'm living in the old Martin place on Amanda Street. I get off at eleven and I'll see you there. That is, if you're still awake."

"How about food? Can I stop at a grocery and pick up some supplies?"

"I stopped by the Red Owl before work, got everything we need. It'll be your turn next week." With that Shirley ran off, disappearing into the kitchen behind the bar.

As I weaved my way through the maze of tables toward the door, I heard a booming guffaw that transcended the laughter from the rest of the bar crowd. Blades Larue stood behind the bar, holding court with a half dozen customers busy downing draught beers and trading jokes. Blades hadn't changed either.

He was a barrel-chested man with a penchant for bawdy stories and fist fights with customers who drank too much and got out of hand. I would have guessed Blades to be in his early fifties, but he looked like he could still skate with the best in the NHL. The only noticeable changes from his playing days were strands of white crowding into his jet-black hair, and a mustache grown to cover scars over his upper lip where more than one hockey puck, and a few fists, had left their marks. When it came to bar fights, though, Blades had a reputation for giving far better than he got.

As I passed the bar a couple of male heads swung my way, always a nice ego boost. One of the group, a tall thin man in a bright red shirt, was delivering the punch line of a joke that got the whole group going again, with Blades' laugh once more booming above the rest.

I would have stopped to tell a few myself, but Mick was waiting patiently in the car.

17

Mick deserved a treat.

He had stayed cooped up in my car for almost two days without uttering so much as a bark or whimper. I stopped at the IGA on the way to Shirley's and picked up a pound of hamburger to mix with his dry dog food. It cost forty-three cents and seven of the sixty-four red ration stamps I was allotted for meat each week, but he was worth it.

Like every other U.S. citizen, I was issued two books of food ration stamps every month. The blue ones were for canned goods like vegetables and soups. You used the red stamps for meat, fish and dairy products. The number of stamps you surrendered for each item often varied from month to month depending on the supply.

Believe me, it could get very confusing.

While Mick was eating, I unpacked my suitcases and put the clothes in the large dresser in the spare bedroom Shirley had reserved for me. She was a great hostess; I could tell by the fresh smell of the sheets and pillowcases that she had made up the bed that morning. Fortunately I was quick, because when I put the last of my blouses in the drawer and turned around, there was Mick waiting with those pleading eyes.

I was due at G.P.'s for dinner in ten minutes, but I couldn't just run out on woman's best friend. I let Mick out the back door into Shirley's large fenced-in backyard and took a seat on her wooden porch. I watched him run around, stopping here and there to sniff at something. Mick has only three legs, but gets around as well as most dogs with all four.

Two years ago I had gotten a phone call from my friend Jim Schiro, a veterinarian who volunteers his services at the local animal shelter near my home. A young German Shepherd had been hit by a car, his right rear leg shattered. The dog's owners had brought him to the shelter to be put to sleep. Jim was confident the leg could be successfully amputated and the dog would live, surviving on three appendages, but the owners balked at having a three-legged pet.

Dr. Schiro knew of my penchant for taking in animals that no one else seemed to care about. Did I want this dog?

Of course I did. I took Mick home after the operation and we've been pals ever since. Since the start of the war, it has become much more popular to refer to dogs of Mick's breed as Alsatians rather than *German* Shepherds. While the name change has become popular in some circles, Mick seems oblivious to the distinction.

After a couple of minutes he came back with a stick in his mouth and dropped it in front of me. Our game. I picked up the stick and threw it overhand toward the rear of the yard. Mick was off before it left my hand, and back in seconds with the stick clutched in his jaws. The loss of a leg certainly didn't bother him; why should it bother anyone else?

I threw it again and again, enjoying the game as much as Mick. He had been my closest companion since Ronny's death, and had been there for me when I needed a friend. He seemed to know something had gone terribly wrong and stood by me.

I had poured myself into my work and it seemed to help lift my spirits somewhat. At the *Times*, I got myself assigned to the police beat where I busted my butt tracking down stories like the current one that almost got me killed. But my real ambition still lay in becoming a foreign correspondent like Edward R. Murrow or Ernie Pyle. This war would decide the direction the world took for the rest of the century and American GIs were fighting for their lives in places like Guadalcanal, Tangiers and Samar. The real stories were there alright, but they wouldn't let a dame anywhere near the actual shooting. And you could bet the money you spent on your last war bond that I wasn't going to travel halfway around the world just to sit in some office interviewing a colonel who hadn't been within a hundred miles of the action, and didn't know an M1 from a B24.

So here I was in northern Michigan. Unable to cover the biggest story of the century, and hiding from the little action my investigative reporting in Detroit had stirred up. For the next month at least my world seemed limited to working for a small town daily paper and playing stick with Mick.

Mick apparently realized I had lost interest in our game. Instead of chasing the stick that I threw, he sat there looking up at me with those big brown eyes. At the same time, I heard the telephone ring inside the house.

I was sure it was G.P. wondering where the hell I was.

18

The danger of an attack on the locks had been on my mind since this afternoon and was anxious to get to G.P.'s to find out more.

His house was a white colonial on 14th Avenue, just outside of the Soo's downtown area and within easy walking distance from Shirley's place. It was home to me too during my senior year at Soo High.

My uncle had almost lost the place in the thirties when local retailers cut their advertising budgets to the bone and his newspaper hemorrhaged red ink. In typical G.P. fashion, he had joked about changing the paper's name to the *Soo Mourning News*.

Now that a wartime economy had turned things around and the paper was flourishing, he could afford a much newer, fancier home. But those lean years had made him cautious.

For me, walking into the house was like donning a favorite old sweater: it felt familiar, warm and comfortable. G.P.'s housekeeper, Mrs. Miller, greeted my appearance at the door with a chipper "Hello" and a warm hug. She was a chubby, round-faced Englishwoman in her late forties who wore a smile as easily as the starched white apron that seemed constantly wrapped around her portly waist. She had served as my uncle's housekeeper since Aunt Susan died over a decade ago, and had been with G.P. just a few months when I showed up for my senior year. She seemed to understand the problems of a seventeen-year old whose parents were going through a contentious divorce and took me on as a personal project. She treated me almost as if I were a second daughter to her beloved Felice. Mrs. Miller taught me cooking, sewing and other feminine niceties, trying to make a lady out of me. While I suspect she thought she had fallen short in that regard, the skills she taught still serve me well living on my own. I bake a mean roast beef and Yorkshire Pudding.

"How's Felice?" I asked Mrs. Miller. "Still east with her father?"

"Lord, no," she answered. "Felice is right here in town. Lives in a flat over on Bingham Street. She's working at Blades LaRue's restaurant as a cook. Speaking of which, dinner's nearly ready. The men are in the den.

"I'll bring you a cocktail."

"Scotch and water, please. With a twist of lemon?"

Mrs. Miller ducked back into the kitchen and I started down the hallway toward the den.

19

I found my uncle and Crawford seated in the den; both rose to greet me as I entered the room.

"Thanks for coming, Kate," G.P. said. As he walked over to give me a hug, I could smell his favorite Old Spice aftershave. "I apologize for not being more cordial this afternoon. You caught us rather by surprise."

"I should be apologizing, G.P. I'm the one who sneaked up on you."

"Good evening, Miss Brennan." I turned to greet Jack Crawford and shake his hand, again impressed by its size and the firm feeling of his grip.

My uncle motioned to a sofa across the coffee table from the chairs that he and Crawford had been using and we all sat down.

"Kate," he began, "it would be impossible to overemphasize the importance of keeping what you heard this afternoon to yourself."

As if to underscore how difficult secrecy could be, Mrs. Miller popped around the corner holding a glass of Scotch and water and halting conversation for the moment.

I thanked her, took a sip and set the glass on a table coaster as she left the room.

"You can count on me to keep a secret, G.P.. But what about the people planning to attend the dedication? If there's real danger of an attack, shouldn't they be warned?"

"Yes, and they will be when the time comes."

"Why all the secrecy until then?"

G.P.'s brow furrowed. "Kate, how much do you know about Enigma?"

"Just that it's the German code no one's been able to break."

G.P. looked at Crawford, then back at me. "If my hunch is right, the Brits have somehow cracked the code."

"That would be great news," I said. "It would put us a step ahead of the Krauts with everything they tried."

"That's right," G.P. said. "But it would be tremendously important not to let them know we'd cracked their code. If they did, they'd change the code and we'd lose the advantage."

Crawford nodded. "That's why I'd hate to be in Churchill's shoes."

That seemed a strange thing to say. "Why is that?" I asked.

Crawford took a drink from his glass before he answered. "The German Luftwaffe is raining bombs on English towns. If the Brits have cracked the code, they know perfectly well when and where the raids are coming."

"Jack's right," said G.P.. "If you're Churchill and you know where they're coming, evacuating the towns would tell the Krauts you've broken their code."

"I'm sure it haunts him every night," said Crawford.

"But what good is the breaking the code if you can't use the information?" I asked.

"If the Brits broke the code," Crawford said, "and it's a big if ... the information they gather would be used on every battle front the Allies are involved in."

"That's right," said G.P.. "Details in areas like troop strength, weaponry and strategy would be priceless."

I was stunned and started to speak, but G.P. held a finger over his lips for silence. Mrs. Miller was coming down the hall again.

"Dinner's ready," she said, peeking around the corner.

I had lost my appetite.

20

I left G.P.'s house soon after supper. All the driving I'd done over the past two days had wrung me out and my body craved sleep. There was a full moon, which made the walk in the darkness of the night's blackout drill much easier.

I didn't see Shirley that evening, and saw little of her the entire weekend. She spent both days working at Blades' restaurant.

Time went quickly as I settled into my new surroundings. The room Shirley had assigned to me was twenty by twenty or so, big enough for a double bed, a chest of drawers with an attached mirror and a comfortable chair. The closet had more than enough space for my clothes. My two empty suitcases went up into the attic.

I walked the four blocks downtown on Saturday, enjoying the sunny day and checking out shops and restaurants to see if things had changed much since my senior year at Soo High. And since the Army had moved in a little over a year ago. I noticed a number of familiar faces, and stopped for short conversations.

There's something special about a small town. People you don't even know smile and say hello as you pass on the sidewalk. I had forgotten how much I missed that openness living in a big city. There were plenty of new buildings but the main difference was in the population. Soldiers seemed to be everywhere: on the sidewalks of Ashmun and Portage Avenue, shopping at Montgomery Ward and J.C. Penny's and crowding into the American Ice Cream Parlor next to the Soo Theatre. Their presence gave me a bit more confidence that a Nazi attack could very well wreak more havoc on the Germans than on the locks.

If G.P. and Crawford had been correct about the possibility of a raid, hopefully they were just as right about the chances of repelling it.

I stopped at a newsstand outside the Ojibway Hotel and picked up a copy of the *Soo Morning News*. The front page was heavy with news of the Allies chasing the Nazis across northern Africa. The sports section reported the woes of the Detroit Tigers who, with their best player Hank Greenberg in the Army Air Force, seemed resigned to going through the motions in a season of mediocrity.

But those stories had come off the wire services. I wanted to read the local news, the work of the News staff. There was plenty of it, and from the stories I read, my uncle's paper still held its own among small town dailies. The reporting for the most part was excellent.

I spent most of the next day kind of lazing around the house. Shirley arrived home that evening just after ten to find me in the bedroom. I had been listening to a broadcast of Fred Allen's *Texaco Star Theatre* that featured Brooklyn Dodger player/manager Leo Durocher. Hearing Durocher talk about the Dodgers' current success made me feel even worse about the Tigers' doubleheader loss earlier in the day.

The sun had gone down and a floor lamp beside the chair and a lamp on the table beside my bed provided the light. Mick lay on the floor at the foot of the bed, his head resting on his paws. Shirley had brought a six-pack of Pfeiffer's home from Blade's place and popped open a beer for each of us. I sat cross-legged on the bed; Shirley lay across the overstuffed chair, legs dangling over the side, foot pumping to the strains of the Andrews Sisters' *Boogie Woogie Bugle Boy of Company B*.

It was as if we were teenagers again.

21

Shirley told me she had heard about Ronny, and expressed condolences, saving me the pain of going through a story I had already told far too many times.

Soon, we were talking about the "good old days:" boyfriends, girlfriends and our teachers at Soo High. The conversation flowed easily and I was beginning to relax. I started to light up a Rameses, an off-brand of cigarette, when I noticed Shirley taking a pack of Old Gold from her shirt pocket.

"Where did you get those?" I asked. "All I can seem to find are Rameses or Pacayunes."

Shirley's forehead squeezed into a frown. "Jeeeze. You might as well try smoking a rope."

"Where did you find Old Gold?"

"At the Red Owl."

"All I saw there were Rameses."

"You've got to ask Jack Casey for 'stoopies,'" Shirley said.

"Stoopies?"

"With the good brands so scarce, they stock cigarettes like Chesterfields and Old Golds under the counter. They save them for regular customers. You've got to know how to ask for them." *Boogie Woogie Bugle Boy* ended and Glenn Miller and his band were playing *That Old Black Magic.* Shirley's foot continued to keep time.

She shook a couple of cigarettes out of her pack and, sitting up, offered me one along with a light. I took a deep drag, thankful for a decent smoke.

I also took a pull from my bottle of Pfeiffer's. The evening was exactly what I needed after what I had been through back in Detroit; maybe Miles had been right about my getting away.

Shirley leaned back across the padded arm of the chair and blew a stream of smoke that nearly reached the ceiling. "Tell me something," she said, looking at me with a grin, "Do they ever call you Scoop Brennan downstate at the Times?"

Scoop was the nickname I'd picked up working on the Soo High newspaper.

"Not a chance," I laughed. "No one knows about that, and I'm sure not going to tell anyone. What about you? I don't remember you having any nicknames in high school."

"I didn't. But I had a doozey when I was young."

"What was it?"

"I'm not saying."

"Come on."

"Promise me you won't laugh."

"Promise."

"After my parents died, I lived with my uncle and aunt in Negaunee." Shirley paused to take a sip of Pfeiffer's and a drag from her cigarette. "I was about seven, I guess; I'd have these terrible nightmares. I'd wake up at night and climb in bed with them. It earned me the wonderful nickname of ... Snuggles."

"Snuggles," I laughed.

"You promised you wouldn't do that."

"Sorry. I just can't picture you as a Snuggles."

Shirley smiled in spite of herself. "Things sure seemed simpler when we were kids. We didn't realize how good we had it."

I agreed. "Kids have a way of magnifying their problems. Breaking up with a boyfriend seemed like the end of the world."

"We always had Toad Hall."

The words conjured up an immediate feeling of nostalgia. I hadn't thought about Toad Hall in years. It was our name for an old abandoned cabin deep in the Minneapolis Woods, just outside of town. The name came from the Kenneth Graham novel, *The Wind in the Willows* and the fact we found a toad hopping around inside the place the day we discovered it.

Someone said the tiny cabin didn't look much like a Hall with a capital "H"and that a name like Toad Stool might be more appropriate. Shirley, who had suggested the name Toad Hall in the first place, said Toad Stool sounded like Hell with a capital H.

The name Toad Hall stuck.

The cabin remained dark and cool inside even on hot summer days. The floor was wood and most of the windows were broken, but we didn't care. There were five of us: Shirley, me, Mary Lapinski, Sue McChesney and Ellen Landon: the only ones who knew about Toad Hall. We'd meet there a couple times a week for animated discussions of boys, teachers and parents.

"Whatever happened to the other girls?" I asked. "Do you hear from them?"

Shirley shook her head as she took a last drag on her cigarette and stubbed the butt out on an ashtray on the table beside her chair. "Mary and I exchanged letters for awhile; but you know how it is. It seems we're all too busy living our own lives."

"I'm sorry you and I lost track of each other after high school," I said. "You were headed for the University of Michigan."

"Yeah. But I dropped out in December of my sophomore year. Same old story: I ran out of money."

"That happened a lot in the Thirties," I said. With both of us puffing on cigarettes, the room had gotten smoky. I got up, walked over to the window and pried it open, trying to fan some smoke out into the night with my hand.

Shirley went on. "I worked in a hardware store down in Traverse City, planning to save some money to go back to college. But I wound up here in the U.P. again instead."

"Must've missed the winters and the ten-foot snow drifts."

"Not exactly. I just got tired of the hardware store. I went to work at a restaurant over in Negaunee; stayed there a couple of years. I came back to the Soo last January." Shirley motioned to our bottles which, by now, were both empty. When I nodded, Shirley grabbed my bottle and went out to the kitchen, coming back with two full Pfeiffer's.

"What's your story, Kate?" she asked as she handed me a beer. "What brings you back?"

I went through the details of my ordeal with the punk on the porch and Miles' insistence that I leave town. Then I told Shirley about my uncle's reluctance to welcome me to the Soo.

"Say, that's not surprising," Shirley said with a wave of her free hand. "Why, with all these GIs here . . . it's not a great place for a young woman in her uncle's eyes."

"What do you mean not a great place?" I said. "You're here with all these GIs."

"I said in her uncle's eyes," Shirley laughed. "In my eyes it's a great place to be." That started me laughing, too.

"Have you met Scotty Banyon?" I asked. "He seems like a great catch for any girl."

Shirley turned serious. "Stay away from him," she said. "He's bad news."

"Why do you say that?"

Shirley paused a moment, then shook her head. "Just stay away."

Her reaction surprised me. I steered the conversation away from Scotty but I couldn't get Shirley's comment out of my mind. Were they dating at one time? Had she been in love? Had he broken off their relationship?

We finished our beer and called it a night soon after twelve o'clock. I had no trouble dozing off.

Looking back, the evening had been so comfortable and the conversation so natural that I never would have guessed it would be the last Shirley and I would ever spend together.

22

Monday, June 21
20 days before the dedication

I made sure I showed up early for my first day of work, and dressed to kill. I wore a red pants suit that had begged me to take it off the rack at Crowley's. I completed the look with a red purse and a pair of red shoes that I figured would knock their eyes out.

Little did I know that my outfit would be upstaged by the news story of the year out of Detroit.

As I strode into the *Morning News* office I spotted Andy Checkle, the young man I had talked to the day before, and walked over to say good morning.

"This one's yours," he said pointing to the wooden desk facing his. "Crawford wanted me to tell you . . . and to help you get situated. He's over at the new MacArthur Lock checking things out. Said he'd be in a little late."

"Thanks." I set my red purse on the desk.

"Say, what do you think about those riots?" Andy asked.

Riots? What riots? "What are you talking about?"

"The race riot in Detroit; started last night on Belle Isle. It's all on the AP wire." Andy pointed to a paper scroll on his desk that had been torn from the Associated Press news wire.

I picked it up and read. Negro and white youths had battled each other the past evening on Belle Isle, the popular island retreat for Detroiters' summer picnics and softball games. White sailors from the nearby Naval Armory had joined in the melee on the side of the white youths and police had been called to restore order.

Racial tensions had been simmering in Detroit for some time, but it was hard to believe that it would deteriorate into a confrontation like this.

I decided to phone Wells Mayburn at the *Times*; I hadn't spoken to my city editor since I arrived at the Soo. His extension was busy, so the switchboard put me through to Jim Russell who manned a desk in the city room two down from mine.

"Jim, what the devil is going on down there?"

"The whole city's in an uproar, Kate. The fighting that started on Belle Isle has spread downtown. The cops are trying their best to cool things down, but they can't be everywhere.

"It's gotten completely out of control, Kate, and there are rumors that Negro leaders are asking Mayor Jeffries to call in federal troops to restore order."

My first day on the job and I was sure I'd be covering a huge story.

Even if it was for a small town paper three hundred miles from the action.

23

"Say, is Crawford going to hit the roof," Andy said as I hung up the phone.

"What are you talking about?" I looked at my watch. "I was here early; it's a quarter of eight."

Andy pointed at my legs. "Those," he said. "Crawford doesn't allow women to wear slacks in the office." Looking around the newsroom, I saw five other women; all wearing dresses or skirts. I also noticed they were looking my way. My slacks suit had drawn attention, but not the kind I wanted.

"Oh, yeah? We'll see about that," I said. It had taken me a month and a half to talk the *Times* brass into letting women wear slacks in the Detroit office. I didn't plan to roll over and play dead for Crawford my first day on the job.

My show of defiance backed Andy off, though. "Sorry," he said, standing up. "I should have kept my mouth shut. Say, it's not my rule; it's Crawford's. Personally, I think your slacks are swell, and Crawford's out of date. This *is* the Forties, after all. Why, women are doing men's jobs everywhere." His face suddenly turned red. "Not that you're a man ... I mean, it's just that..."

"I know what you mean," I smiled. "No harm done."

Andy found me an unused Royal typewriter along with some paper and pencils, which I placed in the top drawer of my desk. He also brought us coffee from the pot on the table against the wall. Soon we were both sitting, facing each other, sipping from our cups. It didn't take long for the conversation to turn to the war.

"Do you think General MacArthur's going to return to the Philippines like he said he would?" Andy asked.

"I wouldn't bet against him," I said. "It took an order from President Roosevelt to get him to leave Corregidor. He didn't want to desert his troops."

"I just wish I were over there somewhere," Andy said. "I would be if it weren't for these." He pointed to the thick lenses in his wire-rimmed spectacles. His eyesight, or lack of it, had no doubt kept him out of the service. If he lost those glasses in combat he'd likely wind up shooting his own men. "I came darn close to getting in."

I took another look at those lenses. "You're kidding."

"Ron Berry, a guy I grew up with, is stationed at Fort Brady," Andy said. "Works near the office where they give the physicals. I talked him into writing down the sequence of letters on the eye exam chart. I memorized them."

"Oh?"

"I took off my glasses and read the chart like I was 20/20," he said.

"So you fooled them?"

"Not exactly. How was I to know they had switched charts?"

"What happened?"

"The Doc played along for awhile. Told me I didn't need glasses and wouldn't give them back."

"So?"

"What could I do? I finally headed for the door."

"And?"

"I walked into a broom closet. They retested me on a new chart and I wound up 4-F."

"Tough luck," I said, holding back a smile.

"Aw, you think it's funny, too. Everybody does. I just wish people could see things my way. No pun intended."

"There are ways other than the Army to serve your country," I said.

"I suppose that's true." Andy looked down at his coffee cup then back to me. "I just wish I could do more here. Every time there's an assignment that means anything Crawford gives it to one of the older reporters. I get stuck writing about weddings, funerals and errant barrage balloons."

"Errant barrage balloons?"

"Happens every once in a while. The wind gets hold of them and they break those cables and float away. They found one downstate in

Cheboygan just this past May."

"No kidding?" I couldn't help feeling sorry for the young guy. He seemed smart enough. Like a lot of bright young people he just needed a chance to show what he could do.

"Why can't I cover stories like the fellow who just got shipped home from the front?" he said. "Gary Hawes. I went to high school with him. He was wounded at the Kasserine Pass. That story's a sure bet to make the front page and I should get the assignment. But I'll probably wind up writing about Mrs. Brinkwater's gardenias."

"Gardenias? Who cares about Gardenias?"

Before Andy could answer my question the front door swung open and Jack Crawford came in off the street. "Morning, Brennan," he called across the room. "C'mon into my office. I've got an assignment for you."

24

I looked at Andy, but he just shrugged. I chose a pencil and a tablet from the stash he had given me and walked across the newsroom into Crawford's office. As I entered, he was removing his hat and suit coat and hanging them on a pole against the window. Had he noticed my slacks outfit?

"Sit down, please," he said, motioning to one of the two chairs in front of his desk. I sat, crossing my legs directly in front of him. My slacks stuck out like a red flag, but Crawford said nothing. He sat down at his desk and rolled up both sleeves. I opened the notebook and waited for him to begin.

Would the assignment involve the race riot downstate? Or perhaps the new McArthur Lock? Or would I draw the job of interviewing the soldier just shipped home from the front?

"Gardenias," Crawford said simply.

"I beg your pardon?"

"Gardenias. You know . . . the flowers?"

"What about them?" *Flowers? What did flowers have to do with my assignment?*

"Apparently Mrs. Viola Brinkwater is known all over the Upper Peninsula for her gardenias. They're extraordinary."

"I'm sure they are. But..."

Crawford held up his hand. "Your uncle told me that every year about this time the paper does a feature story on Mrs. Brinkwater's gardenias. How she grows them, her latest gardening awards ... that sort of thing."

"You want me to write that story." The way I said it sounded like a statement, not a question.

"Yes I certainly do."

"Mr. Crawford . . . are you aware of what's going on downstate?

There's a serious riot happening right now in Detroit."

"Yes, I know. We have all wire service stories and we're using them."

"But what about a local angle? I know people in Detroit, both white and Negro. I can give us some local sidebars."

Crawford let out a sigh. "Miss Brennan, I know perfectly well what's happening in Detroit. But this is Sault Ste. Marie; we're three hundred miles away."

"But it's news."

Crawford held up a hand. "And we're reporting it, thanks to the Associated Press and United Press wire services."

Crawford wasn't going to let me cover the action in my own hometown, but I felt I had to persuade him to let me write about something other than gardenias.

"What about Gary Hawes, the guy who was just shipped home from the Kasserine Pass?" I asked. "That's going to be a great article."

"I agree," Crawford said. "I'm giving it to Chuckles . . . er, Andy Checkle. He went to high school with the kid. Knows him well. Besides he's worked hard and deserves a break."

I swallowed hard. "I think he'll do a swell job," I said. And meant it.

"Here's Mrs. Brinkwater's telephone number," Crawford tore a sheet of paper from the notebook in front of him and handed it across the desk. "She's expecting your call."

I took the paper and got up, heading for the door, when Crawford's voice rang out again.

"By the way, Brennan. About those slacks. . ."

I whirled to face him, ready for a fight. "What about them?"

"They look great on you."

I nearly fell over.

25

I reached Mrs. Brinkwater by phone and, discovering that her daughter was in town visiting, I arranged to meet her for an interview the next day.

I spent the morning in the *News* office watching reports from Detroit coming in over the wire, learning my way around the office and getting to know the people who worked here.

Andy Checkle proved to be a great help, showing me where supplies were stored and introducing me to the staff, including two of the four News reporters. I spoke with Carol Olson and Mary Nelson; the other two were out on assignment.

I wrote a couple of articles on local affairs. Pretty dry stuff.

I stopped at the Red Owl on the way home and picked up some groceries: a pound of pork chops, potatoes, chicken, broccoli and milk. I broiled two of the pork chops, baked a potato and steamed the broccoli on the stove. Mick was my sole dinner companion. Shirley had said she wouldn't be home until after eleven, and would eat her supper at the restaurant.

I listened to the radio as I washed dishes. The news from Detroit wasn't encouraging. More than 6,000 federal troops were spread over the entire city, virtually shutting it down. Governor Kelly had issued orders closing down all restaurants, taverns and movie houses. Still, pockets of violence flared.

Two rumors fueled the flames of hate. One flourished in Paradise Valley, home of much of Detroit's Negro population. A man identifying himself as a policeman told patrons of one nightclub that whites had thrown a colored woman and her baby off the Belle Isle bridge the night before.

Another rumor that a Negro man had raped a white woman on the bridge stirred whites into a frenzy.

As I finished the dishes I noticed that Mick had walked over to the back door and was looking at me. I knew what he wanted, so I opened the door and followed him into the backyard. It took him about fifteen seconds to locate a stick of appropriate size and drop it at my feet. I flung it as far as I could and our game was on. Playing stick with Mick seemed exactly what I needed to get my mind off the madness in my beloved hometown.

After fifteen minutes or so, Mick was worn out. I could tell by the way he dropped the stick twenty feet or so away, instead of bringing it to me. He'd let the stick drop and lay there panting, giving himself a chance to rest.

That was fine with me. I went into the house and turned the radio back on. I needed a break from the insanity going on downstate so I tuned in Jack Benny instead of the news. His humor was just what the doctor ordered, and I found myself actually laughing out loud.

I went to bed at 9:30, leaving a light on in the living room for Shirley.

26

I awoke in the darkness, a feeling of uneasiness washing over me. I switched on the lamp by my bed and saw that the alarm clock on the table beside it pegged the time at quarter after one. I sat upright, and noticed light streaming in from under the door.

Pulling the covers off, I got up and walked quickly out into the hall, Mick trailing behind. The single light I had left burning in the living room was still blazing.

"Shirley?"

I called again. Nothing.

Shirley might have stayed at the restaurant for a drink at the bar, but somehow I didn't think so. She had said rather emphatically that she'd be home right after work.

Something was terribly wrong. I could feel it in my stomach.

I dressed quickly and, leaving Mick to guard the house, I began walking the few blocks to Blades' place.

As I neared the restaurant, I noticed that a crowd of thirty people or so had gathered around the front door. I started running. I pushed my way through the people, but was stopped by a sheriff's deputy at the door. I flashed my *Soo Morning News* card and my worst fears were confirmed when I asked him what had happened.

"Shirley Benoit was stabbed," he said. His red eyes told me the attack had probably been fatal. In a town the size of Sault Ste. Marie everyone knows everyone.

"She's in the alley out back."

27

You might think that working the police beat for a big city paper like the *Times* would cause you to be blasé about a murder scene.

You might think that, but you'd be dead wrong. Every murder scene has its own gristly personality: a bashed head, a knife embedded in the corpse, the exit wound of a bullet that makes you swear off eating for two days.

The difference in this case was the body: the corpse of my best friend lay sprawled beneath a canvas cover on the cement of the alley behind Blades LaRue's. Yellow headlights from two police cars pushed their way through the darkness, illuminating the walls of the buildings on both sides of the alley. A sheriff's deputy knelt beside Shirley's body, holding up the edge of the canvas cover while a large, white-haired man who appeared to be in his late fifties held a flashlight. He seemed to be concentrating on her upper torso; from where I stood I couldn't detect exactly what he saw.

The shock of seeing my friend that way hit me like a cement block dropped from a ten-story building, and I must have looked it. One of the deputies came over and took hold of my arm.

"You can't stay here, Miss." He motioned toward Shirley with his head. "There's been a murder, and the area is off limits to the public."

I tried to speak, but the words stuck in my throat. I fumbled around in my purse and pulled out the *Morning News* card. My hand shook as I held it up to him.

The deputy took the card and, shining his flashlight on it, examined it quickly and handed it back. "Okay, Miss Brennan, but you'll have to stand over there." He pointed toward a small crowd of people at the back doorway of Blade's Saloon. "We're waiting for Doc Larsen to complete his examination. I imagine he'll make an official statement once he's done over here."

28

My mouth dry, my knees weak as straw, I managed to walk the twenty feet to where the crowd stood. The only light, beside the headlamps of the police cars, was coming from inside the bar. I guessed the people here were mostly locals who happened to be in the bar, a couple of them held half full glasses of beer. I noticed Blades looking somber and edged my way toward him.

"Poor Shirley." He shook his head as he spoke. "No one deserves to die like that. Not the way she did."

My thoughts were still reeling, but somehow the reporter instinct deep inside me began to fight its way to the surface. "Did anyone see it happen?"

Blades shrugged his shoulders. "We heard a scream, that's all. It wasn't Shirley who screamed; it was Ellen Popowitz, the other waitress on duty. She had just walked out the back door here for a cigarette break and saw . . . saw. . ." He pointed toward the dark shape on the pavement.

As he did, the man examining Shirley's body stood up and ambled over to the deputy I had just talked to. As shaken as I was over the death of my best friend, I was also a reporter, and I decided to approach the two figures. The way the older man looked at me as I walked toward him told me I'd better introduce myself.

"I'm Kate Brennan, Doctor. I'm a reporter for the Soo Morning News. People are going to want to know what happened here tonight. Can you give me a statement for our next edition?"

Doc Larsen stood a head taller than me, and had the bulk to go with his big frame. Even in the darkness I could see he wore a tired look that said he'd rather be anywhere but in this alley conducting an examination on the body of a young woman who had grown up in the community and he had probably known well. His forehead wrinkled and his lips pursed as he began to speak. He obviously wanted to be precise in any comments made to a news organization. His words were crisp and professional.

"The cause of death was a knife wound to the throat," he said. "A sharp blade severed her left carotid artery and thorax. Death came quickly . . . within seconds."

The deputy spoke up before I had a chance. "So she was stabbed?"

The doctor shook his head. "The wound is not consistent with a stabbing," he said. "The blade moved left to right across her throat. It slashed rather than stabbed. The killer most likely approached her from the rear, surprising her. From the angle of the wound I would guess he was several inches taller than Shirley and right handed."

"How can you be so sure?" I asked.

"There are contusions on her upper torso consistent with being handled roughly. The blade entered the left side of her neck. If the killer held her from behind, and I'm convinced he did, he held her tightly with his left hand, while slashing her with his right.

"I'm sorry. I knew Miss Benoit well. She was a friend." He wiped his eyes with the sleeve of his jacket as he walked away.

29

Claus Krueger sat alone in the darkness of his bedroom, the light from a solitary lamp casting its glow along the blue and yellow pattern of the papered wall.

He had gotten away cleanly. No one had seen him as he slashed the woman. He had watched her start to leave the restaurant through the rear door as he had seen her do every night for the past week. He followed just closely enough to grab her from behind as the door slammed shut in back of them. She had struggled, of course, but in the dark alley the kill had been quick and silent. A woman had passed him as he walked back through the restaurant and he had heard her scream from the backdoor. The patrons were too busy rushing toward the rear of the building to notice him stroll toward the front.

After that it was a simple matter to walk the few blocks back to his home.

He had been suspicious of the woman's real identity almost from the time they met. It became obvious after awhile that she was equally suspicious of him and his reasons for being in Sault Ste. Marie. When she began probing deeper, she left him no choice.

Krueger got to his feet and turned the lamp toward him, looking at himself in the mirror above the dresser. The left sleeve of his black shirt was caked with blood. The woman's struggle had forced him to hold her firmly while he sliced her throat. Blood had spurted immediately, but he had been clever in wearing the dark shirt. The restaurant light was turned low and no one noticed the blood stains as he walked back through the crowd of customers clamoring for the back door.

He removed the shirt as he walked to the bathroom. A twist of the tap started cold water running into the bowl. He dipped the shirt under the faucet, holding it in the stream of cold water. The water turned pink and then dark red as it left the shirt and ran into the bowl and down the drain. He wrung the shirt in his hands again and again, each time opening it to soak up more cold water. Finally the water was clear; the final vestiges of Shirley Benoit had disappeared down the drain.

The shirt would be discarded of course. The washing was a temporary, cautionary measure. Tomorrow he would bury the evidence in the backyard.

Satisfied for now, Krueger returned to the bedroom, removed his pants and folded them on a chair. He turned off the lamp and in the darkness pulled back the covers and climbed into the bed.

It had been an eventful evening.

30

Tuesday, June 22

I slept no more than four hours that night, tossing and turning in my bed. Why Shirley? Why did she have to die? Why my oldest and dearest friend in the Soo? I hoped somehow I'd wake up and find it had all been a nightmare.

Shirley's parents had both passed away when she was young and she lived with her grandmother during the time I knew her. At one time she had also lived with an aunt and uncle somewhere in the Upper Peninsula, and the sheriff's people were trying to track them down.

Tuesday morning I stood outside the sheriff's office and Sault Ste. Marie jail. I clenched and unclenched my fists, a knot the size of a walnut twisting in the pit of my stomach. One part of me wanted desperately to turn and walk away. I didn't cherish the idea of meeting the man who police said killed my best friend.

But the seasoned reporter inside me won out; I'd go in. I had interviewed dozens of accused killers back in Detroit and tried to visualize this as one more job.

The lobby was sparsely appointed: a wood floor, bare white walls and three desks that appeared as if they had been in place since the turn of the century. An American flag and the blue Michigan flag set on stands against the far wall, pictures of President Roosevelt and Governor Kelly adorned the wall between them.

The personnel had changed since I had lived here years ago. Sheriff Bergen had retired and a new man had taken his place. The deputy at the desk nearest the door looked up as I entered. He appeared to be in his early sixties, with a shock of white hair and a ruddy complexion. The belly that hung well over his belt challenged the buttons of his tan police uniform to their limits, and his pants had long ago lost their crease. His shoes looked as if he had shined them with a chocolate bar.

"I'm from the Soo Morning News," I said. "I'm here to talk to the soldier you have in custody."

"I've got a lot of soldiers in custody."

"This one is here because of the stabbing."

"You're from the News?" He looked skeptical. "What happened to Jack Crawford and Ben Donaldson? They're the ones usually show up here."

"I'm new." I reached into my purse for my press card. "My name is Kate Brennan."

The press ID seemed to do the trick. "I'm Deputy Ericksen, Miss Brennan." He stood up and reached for a set of keys resting on a hook against the wall. "So, you want to see the colored boy involved in last night's stabbing?"

"The Negro soldier, yes. I'm here to interview him. It's official newspaper business."

"All right. This way, please."

31

I followed Deputy Ericksen toward a door in the rear of the lobby. He looked back over his shoulder. "I can't let you in the cell, but you can talk to him through the bars."

"He's not armed. What's the danger?"

"Policy, ma'am. He's under arrest for murder."

He took a few more steps, stopped and turned to me, saying softly, "Don't tell the sheriff I said so, but he don't seem the type to be here. We see some of the same faces every week or so. But far as I can tell, this fella's never been in trouble before."

"Why is he here, then?"

"You heard what's going on in Detroit? The rioting and all? Well, couple of the deputies thought the stabbing of a white woman might be some sort of retaliation for the arrests and beatings of the colored down there.

"They found him walking alone, after the Army curfew. They said he didn't seem to know where he was or where he was going. Or care."

"And that makes him a murder suspect?"

The deputy shrugged. "Well, he's all we've got." He turned and resumed walking.

We passed through the door at the back of the lobby and into a narrow hallway, my heels tapping against the wooden floor. Doors were closed on either side of the hall, but I could see a large room at the end. As we entered, my nose caught the smell of urine covered up with Spic and Span. There were three separate cells, one held four white prisoners, another five Negro soldiers. The third cell housed a single Negro soldier who sat on the bottom of a double bunk. He looked up as we neared the cell.

"Cummins, this lady's from the Morning News. Wants to talk to you." He turned to me. "I'll give you ten minutes." I watched as he retraced his steps down the hallway, shoes beating time, echoing against the narrow walls.

I turned to find the prisoner had stood. Roy Cummins was a light-skinned Negro just short of six feet in height. He wore a corporal's uniform, wrinkled as if he had slept in it, which he undoubtedly had. But his shoes bore a mirror finish that reflected light. He approached me, putting his hands on the bars, but remained silent.

"My name is Kate Brennan," I said. "I'm a reporter."

His brow wrinkled. "Yes, ma'am. Do I have to talk to you?"

"No. You don't."

"Then why should I?"

"For openers, there's a race riot tearing a city to shreds downstate. And there's a whole town of people up here who think you murdered a young woman. If there's a side to your story, this is your chance to tell it."

"With all due respect, ma'am, I don't care what your town thinks."

This wasn't going to be easy.

32

I reached into my purse and retrieved a pack of Chesterfields I had bought a half hour ago at the Red Owl. I offered one to Cummins, who took it, and I put one in my mouth. I lit mine and handed him the lighter.

I inhaled deeply and blew out a stream of smoke. "Sault Ste. Marie isn't my town," I said. "I came up here from Detroit."

He lit his cigarette and handed back the lighter. "Detroit?"

"I was a reporter for the Times."

"I know the Times. I grew up in Detroit."

"You must have heard about the rioting going on down there?"

Cummins, looking at the floor, nodded his head. "Started on Belle Isle and spread all over town. The police seem to be arresting a lot of colored people; not many whites."

It was true. "That's what happens when most of the police are white," I said.

Cummins looked up at me. "Just like this town."

I decided to change the subject. I asked him which part of Detroit he came from, hoping the small talk would put him at ease. I pulled out a writing pad and began to take notes. Cummins was born near the downtown area, on Hastings Street. His father died when he was just four years old and he was raised by an uncle and aunt. His young mother was forced to work two jobs to support herself and Cummins' two younger siblings. His mother insisted her children attend religious services regularly, and they were all members of nearby First Baptist Church. When he graduated from high school he accepted a football scholarship from Louisiana Negro Normal and Industrial Institute in Louisiana. He earned a three-year teaching certificate and stayed nearby, teaching at a colored high school and working as an assistant on the Institute's football team under their new coach, Eddie Robinson.

"I figured I could do more good in the south," Cummins said. "People down there seem more needful of good teachers than here in the north."

The offer of the cigarette and the conversation had loosened Cummins' tongue. His hands extended through the bars, folded comfortably in front of him as he spoke. He seemed a lot more relaxed than when we began and I figured it was time to pop the sixty-four dollar question. I tried to appear equally nonchalant as I took another drag from my Chesterfield and blew out the smoke.

"Why'd you kill that young woman?"

Cummins reacted as if he had been shot. He leaned backwards suddenly, arms motioning as he spoke. "I didn't kill anyone. I swear it."

"I've hardly ever interviewed a suspect who said he was guilty."

His eyes tightened into a squint. It was as if the pleasant conversation of a moment ago had never taken place. "Look, ma'am. I don't care what you think. Or what this town thinks. But I do care what the fellows in my regiment think. And I didn't kill that woman."

"Where were you around midnight last night?"

Cummins paused, looking down at the cement floor and then back up again to me. "I . . . I left Fort Brady just after 2100 hours. Went for a walk. The cops arrested me on Division Street. It was a little after midnight."

"Three hours. That's a long walk. Where did you go?"

"Here. There. It was just a walk."

"Anyone with you?"

"I was by myself."

"Anyone see you?"

"No, ma'am. No one I knew."

"You're going to have to do better than that."

"That's all I can tell you, ma'am. It's what happened."

It was clear he wasn't going to say anything further. But there was one more thing I needed to check out.

"Before I go," I said, handing him the pad and pencil, "I need you to sign these notes to verify that the facts are correct." He looked at me as if he recognized the lie, then skimmed through the words and signed *with his left hand.*

I was convinced the sheriff was holding the wrong man for murder.

But I was equally sure that Corporal Roy Cummins was holding something back.

33

The time I'd spent with Corporal Cummins had left me confused.

I doubted he was guilty of murder, but there seemed something beneath the surface, something he held close to himself.

As I walked back through the lobby, I found Carol Olson standing at the deputy's desk.

"Hi, Kate, just getting released? Must have been a whopper of a night."

I didn't find the remark humorous. "Just doing a little research," I said. "Talking with Corporal Cummins."

"Why, that's funny," Olson said. "I hope you don't plan on writing anything. I'm covering last night's murder. Crawford gave me the assignment and I'm here to interview Sheriff Valenti."

The words stung, but I tried not to show it. "Great," I said, "I'll be interested to read your story."

When I got to the newsroom, I set my purse on my desk and sat down. I wanted to cool off before confronting Crawford.

I found Viola Brinkwater's telephone number in my notepad and dialed her number. After some preliminary niceties, we agreed on meeting at her home at 10:30.

I looked at the clock. I had just enough time to talk with Crawford before leaving the office for Mrs. Brinkwater and her damned gardenias.

I found him at his desk, reading.

"Why did you assign Carol Olson to the story of Shirley Benoit's murder?" I asked.

Crawford looked up from the papers he was perusing. He obviously wasn't accustomed to having his assignments questioned and looked a bit surprised. "She's one of our best reporters," he said. "Besides you've got another story today."

"Yeah. Viola Brinkwater and her gardenias."

"There are a couple of weddings and a funeral we need written up for tomorrow's edition, too. And don't forget the list of ship passages through the locks."

"Gardenias, weddings, funerals and ships going through the damn locks. A cub reporter could handle those assignments."

That got Crawford's attention. He reared back in his chair. "Look. You can't walk in here off the street and expect to get preferential treatment. Even if you did work at a big Detroit daily."

"The woman who was murdered, Shirley Benoit? She and I were best friends."

"I'm sorry. I didn't know." Crawford paused for a moment; then came back at it. "But, that's even more reason *not* to assign you to the story. Being that close to the victim can sway your judgment."

"My judgment is just fine. Apparently much better than yours."

"Prove it by bringing in a good story on Mrs. Brinkwater's gardenias."

Great. The news story of the century was blazing away overseas, the news story of the year was tearing apart my hometown, and I was in Sault Ste. Marie writing about Viola Brinkwater's fragrant gardenias.

That stunk.

34

I sat upright and much straighter than I wanted to, in a hard wooden chair in the sunroom of Mrs. Viola Brinkwater's brown and white ranch home on Superior Street.

All of eighty years old, Mrs. Brinkwater's pinched face gave her the appearance of one of those people who are most comfortable being uncomfortable. She wore a plain white dress, a perfect match for the gardenias that filled the myriad of planters arranged about the sunroom. Their sweet, distinctive aroma permeated the moist air.

"Thank you for seeing me this morning, Mrs. Brinkwater."

"My pleasure, dearie." Mrs. Brinkwater's mouth cracked into a smile.

"Your gardenias are beautiful."

"Gardenia jasminoides. Thank you."

"You certainly know your gardenias, Mrs. Brinkwater."

"Why, ask anyone in Sault Ste. Marie. They'll tell you no one knows gardenias like I do."

"I'm sure they would."

"Gardenias were discovered in China in the Eighteenth Century."

"And, how long have you been growing them?" *Probably since they were discovered in China.*

"I started as a teenager, actually."

I looked down at my notes. "Tell me, Mrs. Brinkwater, what's the secret of growing beautiful gardenias like these?"

"Coin."

"Coin?"

"C-O-I-N. It's a way of remembering my system. C is for cool nights. Gardenias like fifty to fifty-five degrees. No more. No less."

"I see." I scribbled in the notepad on my lap.

"O is for oxygen. Important to their photosynthesis. The letter I stands for indirect light. You notice my windows are all shaded by an overhanging roof."

"Uh-huh."

"And n... that's for nitrogen in the soil. Put 'em all together and they spell 'coin.'"

"Very clever."

Mrs. Brinkwater looked pleased. "Why, it's known as a mnemonic device, a way of jogging the memory. Daniel taught me to use memory joggers. He was my first husband. Daniel played the piano."

"The piano?"

"Face. F-A-C-E. It's the way students learn the notes between the lines of a musical score."

"And Daniel taught you that?"

"Daniel fingered those keys like a pro. So did my..." she paused momentarily, "... my uh, second husband Alden. There were four, you know. It's difficult sometimes to keep their order straight."

With the interview going nowhere fast, I had just put my pencil in a pocket when Mrs. Brinkwater let go with a sharp epithet that nearly brought me out of the chair.

"Damn!"

"I beg your pardon? Did you say damn?" The old lady must have been losing her marbles.

"No, damm. D-A-M-M. It's the way I remember my husbands." She *was* losing her marbles.

"And how does that work, Mrs. Brinkwater."

"D-A-M-M. It's another mnemonic device, dearie."

I simply nodded.

"The first letter, d, is for Daniel. He was my first husband. Alden was my second. Those are the first two letters of damm."

I nodded again.

"Michael was my third. He's the first m."

"Uh-huh. And the second m?"

"That would be Matthew. Or was it Matthew first and then Michael? They're all gone now, of course. Poor dears."

I sat there dumbly, not believing my ears.

"Now you string those names together ... and it comes out d-a-m-m, damm. It's the way I keep them all in order."

I closed my notebook. The paper would have to survive without its article on Mrs. Brinkwater's gardenias this year.

"Judas Priest, girl. You're impatient. You remind me of my husband Michael. Never could sit still."

"I'm afraid that's me." I stood.

Mrs. Brinkwater went on. "Why, instead of relaxing in the evenings like most sensible men, he'd run whiskey across the border with Roland Swenson. That was a while ago, during Prohibition. Roland's our mayor, you know."

That bit of news got me to sit back down. Rafe Johnson had been mayor when I was in the Soo for my senior year in high school, but I recalled hearing Swenson's name as the mayor before Olson. He must have decided to run again.

"Are you telling me, Mrs. Brinkwater, that the mayor of Sault Ste. Marie once ran illegal whiskey across the Canadian/United States border?"

"With Michael, yes. It's a long story."

"Believe me, Mrs. Brinkwater, I have plenty of time." I cracked open my notebook.

35

I got back to the newsroom anxious to write the article about our mayor and his history of running booze across the border in violation of Prohibition laws, but was interrupted by a phone call.

A man identifying himself as Mr. Rodgers from the L. Rodgers Funeral Home asked if I could provide him with a dress that could be placed on Shirley's body for the funeral service. I agreed to meet him at Shirley's home on Amanda Street during the noon hour.

I had dreaded the thought of going through Shirley's personal effects, but now with no other choice, I met Mr. Rodgers in front of the home a little after twelve.

I let Mick out for a run in the backyard then invited Mr. Rodgers to have a seat in the front room while I went into Shirley's bedroom for the first time since her death.

Shirley's closet was filled with clothes, but most appeared to be too casual. Shirley was a sharp dresser, preferring bright colors to earth tones. The latest garments were made of rayon and some of the other newer artificial fabrics; wools and cottons were hard to come by since they had been restricted for use in military uniforms.

Sadly, it reminded me of all the times as teenagers that Shirley and I would go through each other's closets looking for something to wear to a party or dance. Our sizes were interchangeable and we often borrowed each other's clothes.

Now I was looking for something for my best friend to wear at her own funeral.

After some searching, I found a powder blue wool dress that Shirley must have had for some time. It was ankle length, tied at the waist and featured a collar that could be turned up to hide any wounds on her neck. I pulled it from the closet and carried it out to the living room to show Mr. Rodgers.

"Hmm . . ." he said, running his hands over the garment and turning up the collar, "this will do nicely."

Mr. Rodgers' visit had heightened my feelings of sorrow over Shirley's passing and quelled any appetite I might have had for lunch. I simply returned to the office and wrote the story.

36

"That's me cross-checking Johnny Gottselis in the third game of the '32 Stanley Cup finals."

Blades Larue had noticed me studying one of the black and white photos on the wall behind where he stood wiping glasses. I was sitting at the bar nursing a Budweiser. I had written the story about Mrs. Drinkwater's husband and left the office early. I wanted to ask Blades a few questions about the tragedy of the last evening before the after-work rush hour started.

He was more interested in talking hockey. "The Black Hawks beat us in seven games, but we got back at them in '36. That's when we took the Cup for the first time.

"I retired right after the season and moved up here."

"My father covered the Wings for the Times."

"He did?"

"He probably interviewed you. Buck Brennan?"

"Sure. Buck Brennan was your father? What's your name?"

"I'm Kate Brennan, Blades. We've never met formally, but I've been in here for lunch and supper with my uncle. I used to come up here for a week or two almost every summer."

Blades stopped wiping the glass he was holding. "Kate Brennan. Kate Brennan. Yeah, you're G.P. Brennan's niece. Now I remember." He smiled and resumed wiping. His sleeves were rolled up and his meaty forearms bulged with every move. It was easy to see how a flick of those wrists could send a puck rocketing past a surprised goalie.

"Shirley Benoit and I were best friends."

Blades stopped wiping again. "Shirley was our best waitress. Smartest, too." He shook his head. "It was a crying shame what happened to her."

"Tell me about that night."

Blades put the clean glass down and picked up another from the sink. "Shirley finished her shift at one and left. Ellen Popowitz was closing. A minute or so later, Ellen made sure her tables were happy and walked out there for a cigarette." Blades motioned toward the back door with his head. "That's when she found . . . you know."

"Will Ellen be in later?"

Blades shook his head. "I gave her a couple days off. She's still pretty shook up."

"Did you see anyone in the restaurant that night who might have looked suspicious?"

"In here? Nah. Just the usual amount of locals; and soldiers of course. They're great drinkers, but lousy tippers. I thought they caught the guy who killed her. That Army corporal."

"He's in jail," I said. "But some people think he may not have done it." I didn't elaborate.

Blades set the glass down. "Too bad we don't have the death penalty here in Michigan," he said. "Prison's too good for the son-of-a-bitch who killed Shirley. I wish I could help you find him."

Unfortunately, Blades couldn't. But maybe Ellen Popowitz could.

37

I found Ellen at home in the upstairs flat she rented on Maple Street. She had answered the door and now sat facing me across a coffee table. She was a small woman, slight of build, who looked even smaller huddled in the chair with her legs and arms crossed. It was clear from the redness around her eyes that she had been crying.

"No, I never got a look at whoever killed Shirley," she was saying. "Like I told the deputies, I walked out the door for a cigarette and saw . . . saw Shirley lying there on the ground." She dropped her face into her hands and began sobbing softly.

"I'm sorry to be asking you these questions, Ellen," I said. "But Shirley was a good friend of mine, too. And I think I owe it to her to help the authorities find her killer."

Ellen stopped crying and looked up at me. "What about that colored soldier?"

"Corporal Cummins? He didn't do it."

"But the sheriff . . ."

"Cummins was picked up walking blocks away. If he were the killer he'd have had blood all over him. But he was clean."

"Then why . . .?"

"He's the only suspect they could find."

Ellen covered her face again with her hands. I realized my time with her was going to run out soon.

"Ellen, did you notice any suspicious-looking characters in the tavern last night?"

She shook her head without looking up. "Just the usual crowd. You know: locals and soldiers. I knew most of them; by sight, at least."

Ellen uncovered her face and looked up at me again. "I don't understand. You say that soldier didn't kill Shirley."

"That's right."

"Then, who did?"

"That's what I'm going to find out."

38

Wednesday, June 24

"Your story's not running, and that's final." Jack Crawford slammed the desk with his fist.

"What do you mean it's not running?" I stood in front of that desk, shouting just as loudly. I couldn't believe it. A first-rate story about the mayor running illegal booze across the border during Prohibition had to be the Scoop of the Century in this little burg. And the managing editor was apparently too cautious to run it.

"You won't let me write a legitimate story about a murder or riot. Then, instead of writing some mundane pap about flowers, I bring you a story with some substance and you don't know what to do with it."

"Oh, I know what to do with it," Crawford said. "I'm tossing it in the wastebasket."

"What's the matter? Too controversial?"

"No..."

"Isn't controversy what news is all about?"

"News is all about what's happening."

"Sure. And up here that means garden club meetings, ship passages and who's engaged to whom."

"If that's what's happening, that's what we write. We report the news, we don't manufacture it."

"And you think I manufactured this story? Maybe G.P. will see things differently."

"I doubt it."

"Well let's see about that." I started for the door that separated his office from Crawford's. It was closed but I didn't let that bother me, flinging it open without knocking, a big mistake. G.P. had just hung up the phone. He stood as I approached his desk, and I could tell by the look on his face he wasn't used to reporters barging into his office.

"Yes, Kate, what is it?"

I took that as an invitation to lay out the whole story, rehashing the argument Crawford and I had just been through. I could hear Crawford's footsteps as he entered the office and I could feel him stop just behind me. When I finished, G.P. just stood there shaking his head.

"So you really want me to run this story?" G.P. asked.

"Damn right I do."

"And which sources have you contacted to verify the facts? I mean, other than Mrs. Brinkwater."

"I tried Mayor Swenson, but he wouldn't talk to me."

"That was him on the phone just now."

"Trying to spike the story, I suppose."

"Yes, he was. But not for reasons you're thinking."

I decided to keep my mouth shut and let G.P. explain. It turned out to be one of the smartest things I've ever done.

"Viola Brinkwater is known for her green thumb," G.P. said. "But her touch on reality leaves something to be desired."

"You're saying her husband Michael didn't run illegal whiskey across the border with Roland Swenson during Prohibition?"

"Not exactly. Michael ran illegal whiskey across the border with Roland Swenson, Sr.; everyone knew that. Hell, illegal booze helped get Swenson elected.

"But Roland Swenson, Jr., our current mayor, wasn't even in town back then."

"You mean . . . ?"

"Our current mayor is the son of the man who ran whiskey. He was away at college and serving in the military during most of Prohibition."

So the old bat *was* nutty. I stood there, my mouth open, as G.P. went on. "Viola Brinkwater's husband back then, during Prohibition, was Alden Mathews, her second."

G.P. sat down behind his desk. "I've known Viola Brinkwater for years, Kate. She never could keep her husbands straight."

Damn!

39

"Kate, I need you back in Detroit."

It was Wells Mayburn's voice. His call reached me at my desk where I was still stinging from my conversations with G.P. and Crawford.

"It's the third day of rioting in the city, and things seem to have quieted down somewhat," Wells said. "But what happens next is anybody's guess. You could cut the tension in the air with a knife. So far more than 700 people have been injured. A lot of them badly enough that they're still in the hospital."

Despite my run-in with Crawford, and the temptation to tell him to go to hell and take my job with him, I had to stay. Shirley Benoit was dead, and the authorities had the wrong man in jail.

"I can't leave the Soo, Wells. My best friend has been murdered, and I can't go anywhere without knowing who killed her."

"I heard about a murder up there, Kate, but I didn't know the victim was a friend. I'm sorry. But they've made an arrest."

"Yeah, a false arrest. I'm certain the man they've locked up didn't do it."

"I've never doubted your instincts, Kate. But are you sure you won't reconsider?"

"Sorry, Wells."

"At least tell me you'll think about it, Kate. We're undermanned here. We could really use you."

I couldn't let him get away with that. "Just because you're undermanned, huh?"

"You know what I mean, Kate. You're my best investigative reporter. I want to get to the bottom of these riots. Find out how they started."

"And I need to find out who killed my friend. Sorry, Wells, I'd like to help."

Of all the times for Wells to call, this had to be the absolute worst. Two days ago I would have given my eyeteeth to be back in Detroit, reporting the story of the decade, if not the century. But I couldn't go.

Not now.

40

The evening sun was sinking slowly into Lake Superior's Whitefish Bay, its light glittering out over the waters, turning their dark blue color to a brilliant, blinding white.

I had driven to a spot outside of town where you can watch the sun descend into those icy blue waters and listen to the surf pound onto the beach. I left my car and walked to a spot where I sat cross-legged on a patch of grass near the edge of the sand. With a clump of trees and ferns behind me I felt totally isolated.

I had found solace in this place many times as a high school student after I had done poorly on an exam or broken up with a boy friend. As a group, we girls had our "Toad Hall." But this is where I came when I wanted to be totally alone.

And right now, this is where I had to be, even though it meant a twenty-mile drive that burned a few gallons of precious gasoline.

I had screwed up; done something a cub reporter wouldn't do. I had felt so damn sure of myself, so certain of showing up the locals that I had disregarded the number one rule of journalism: I hadn't checked my sources.

More than that, though, I had forgotten the respect for small town people I had gained during my time in Sault Ste. Marie as a teenager. People in small towns are no dumber or smarter than those of us who happen to live in big cities. They're simply people who have chosen to live their lives away from the noise, traffic and pressure of big city living.

Maybe they're smarter than city dwellers, after all.

At any rate, I knew what I should have done. I should have insisted on talking to the mayor. I should have searched the archives at the library to

verify names and dates. I should have done a dozen things that I simply
didn't do. Instead I rushed the story through my typewriter and took it to
Jack Crawford, giving him the perfect opportunity to show up the big city
reporter.

The jerk. And to think I had found the man attractive when we first
met. How could I have thought that? Even marginally? I despised the smug
way he handled the whole affair. He could have told me the current mayor
wasn't Viola Brinkwater's husband's friend during Prohibition. You can bet
your rear end he knew that. But he let me barge into G.P.'s office and make
a fool of myself.

He could go to hell for all I cared. I'd sit here as long as I felt like it,
taking in a breathtaking view of one of God's most beautiful creations.
Alone.

Just as I began to enjoy the solitude, I heard the crackle of leaves and
twigs breaking underfoot and turned to see a tall, blonde-haired man
making his way through the copse of trees behind me.

It was Scotty Banyon, the man I had met at the locks.

41

I had wanted to see Scotty Banyon again, even if I hadn't been able to totally admit it to myself. But I wasn't eager to see anyone while I was wallowing in self-pity. I tried my best to smile as he approached.

"I thought that was your car parked back out on the road," he said. "I was driving home from the mine when I spotted it. I wanted to be sure you were okay."

"I'm just taking in the beauty of the sand and water," I said.

"I thought you said you were new in town. How'd you know about this place?"

"I spent my senior year of high school in Sault Ste. Marie," I said. "I used to come here quite fre . . . ah, once in a while." Truth is, this was also known as the lovers' lane for kids when I was in high school. I'd been out here my share of times that way, too. But Scotty didn't need to know that.

"Mind if I sit down?"

"Sure, why not." The way I said it, it came out more like a statement than a question. He sat down beside me, leaning back on one hand and brushing a lock of golden hair from his eyes with the other. His eyes were blue, dark blue. Blue like the water in the bay.

"What brings you to the Soo?" Scotty asked. He was dressed in a short-sleeved blue shirt and even in the dim light I couldn't help noticing some pretty fair triceps definition.

"I'm up here on sort of a sabbatical, I guess you could say. I'm a reporter for the Detroit Times downstate. I decided it was time for a break." I certainly didn't want to go into the whole story. "You from the Soo?"

Scotty shook his head. "I'm originally from the Upper Peninsula," he said. "But farther west, toward Wisconsin. Actually, I live out in Arizona now. I have a home near Phoenix. But when I was young my family lived over in Copper Harbor."

"Arizona, huh? You're a long way from home."

"I've been in the Soo for a few months . . . doing some exploratory mining near here."

"Mining? For what, gold?"

"No." A smile creased his face. "Copper." He pointed west. "The western part of the Upper Peninsula used to be full of it."

"That's what I've heard." Copper mining had been a huge part of the U.P. until the first part of the Twentieth Century. "I also heard the mines dried up. What makes you think you'll find more copper now?"

"There's always been copper here, it just got too expensive to mine. The war has changed everything. Now the government needs the metal, and they're willing to pay more for it. Suddenly, mining is profitable again. You just have to go deeper. And find new veins."

"You found one?"

"About twenty miles west of town. We've been blasting out the side of a mountain, and the results look promising."

"How come you know so much about it?"

"My family owned one of the largest mines in Michigan," Banyon said. "When the vein they mined began to run out, my dad decided to close up shop. We moved to Arizona."

"Lucky he saw the proverbial 'hand writing on the wall.' I hear a lot of companies went bust in the Twenties."

Banyon nodded in agreement. He suddenly seemed distracted by his thoughts, looking out over the bay where the sun had now dipped below the horizon, leaving a hint of fire red in the dark sky.

It was time to leave. Scotty stood and offered a hand to help me up. I ignored it and got up by myself. He took a flashlight from somewhere in his jeans and we followed its yellow path through the trees. We crossed the grassy meadow and I could hear crickets chirping everywhere as we approached the road where a gorgeous black Packard dwarfed my Ford.

He seemed reluctant to go, standing in front of his car and running his hand through his hair. "Well, I'll see you around town, I'm sure."

I told him we probably would see each other and we both got into our cars. His lights followed mine for ten miles or so and then turned off on a narrow dirt road.

I didn't realize just how much of Scotty Banyon I'd be seeing.

42

Sheriff's Deputies Nab Killer

Sault Ste. Marie, Wednesday, June 23, 1943 – Sheriff's deputies believe they have arrested the killer of a local woman who was brutally slashed in the alley behind Blades Larue's Restaurant early Tuesday morning.

"We've got the killer alright," said Sheriff Carl Valenti. "My deputies arrested a young Negro soldier they found wandering aimlessly not far from the murder scene at two a.m. He had no excuse for being at that place at that time."

Arrested was Corporal Roy Cummins, 25, of the 100th Artillery Squadron stationed at Fort Brady. The soldier is currently being held without bail in the Sault Ste. Marie jail.

The victim, Shirley Benoit of 875 Amanda Street, was born in the Soo, and had lived here until leaving to attend the University of Michigan. She had held a number of jobs downstate before moving back to Sault Ste. Marie.

The two heroes who made the arrest are Sheriff's Deputies Mel Kristensen and Douglas Hein. Both were extremely modest as they asked questions posed by a Morning News reporter.

Yes, they found the killer walking a dark, deserted street shortly after two this morning. No, they didn't feel their lives were in danger as they approached the man with their guns drawn.

"He made no move to resist arrest," said Deputy Hein. "In fact, he came with us peaceably."

"He didn't seem to know why we were apprehending him," said Deputy Kristensen. "But that's not uncommon among perpetrators who wish to appear *innocent."*

"We're gratified to solve this horrible murder so quickly," said Sheriff Valenti. "I credit it to outstanding police work on the parts of Deputies Kristensen and Hein.

(Story continued on Page 5)

43

Thursday, June 24

I couldn't believe my eyes when I read Carol Olson's story just after the *News* hit my porch the next morning. And I couldn't wait to get to the office to confront her.

When I caught Olson at her desk, I was ready with my sarcastic best.

"Good morning, Carol. Say, I must have missed the trial."

She looked up from her typewriter. "What trial?"

"Why, Corporal Cummins' trial. From your article in this morning's News, he's already been tried and convicted."

Her face grew red. "What do you mean? The story reflected what Sheriff Valenti told me."

"Exactly. But what about Corporal Cummins? Did you speak with him?"

"Well, no . . . "

"And did you speak to the coroner?"

"What about?"

"What about? What about?" Now I couldn't believe my ears, either. "The coroner has said that Shirley Benoit was slashed by a right-handed assailant."

"So?"

"Corporal Cummins happens to be left handed."

"How do you know?"

"I interviewed him in his cell. When the interview concluded, I asked him to read over my notes for accuracy and sign them."

Olson frowned. "Whoever heard of having the subject of an interview sign the reporter's notes?"

"A reporter who wanted to determine whether the prime suspect in a murder committed by a right-handed killer was right or left handed," I said.

"And ..."

"Corporal Cummins is left handed."

"That proves nothing."

"Maybe not. But neither does arresting a person on suspicion of murder just because he happens to be walking in the wrong place at the wrong time. And also just happens to be a man of color."

"You think his race had something to do with it?"

"Don't you? What if he happened to be a well-dressed, middle-aged white man walking that same street?"

Olson's silence answered the question for her. I decided to let her down gently.

"Look, Carol," I said. "We all make mistakes. I made a doozey myself the other day." I purposely didn't elaborate, hoping she hadn't heard about my blunder with Mrs. Brinkwater's husband and the mayor.

The Cheshire cat grin on Olson's face told me she had heard; probably along with the rest of the Allied world.

"You're right," she said. "That was a doozey."

So much for letting her down gently. I wanted to push her hair into the paper slot of her typewriter and turn the cartridge ten revolutions or so.

But instead, I walked away.

44

It had been four days since the incident on Belle Isle ignited a firestorm, and the word from Detroit was that the situation had quieted.

The rioting had taken a toll, especially on the Negro population. Twenty-five persons of color had been killed, compared with nine whites. The estimate of property damage stood at two million dollars.

The news didn't escape the Nazis. Vichy France radio reported that the riot characterized "the internal disorganization of a country torn by social injustice and racial hatred."

I desperately wanted to believe they were wrong. But I knew my country had a long way to go before the words "all men are created equal" applied to every man and woman.

When I got to my desk after my little run-in with Olson, a handwritten message informed me that Scotty Banyon had called just before I walked into the office.

I dialed the number on the message, wondering what he wanted. It didn't take long to find out. He answered on the third ring.

"How about joining me for dinner tonight aboard my boat?" he asked. He said he had purchased a fairly good-sized cruiser earlier in the spring, and it was moored at the Riverbend Marina in the St. Marys River a mile or so east of the locks.

I had mixed feelings about joining Scotty on a "date". It had been little more than a year since Ronny was killed at Midway and I still missed him. A day didn't go by that I didn't think of him.

On the other hand, maybe Scotty was planning nothing more than a pleasant evening aboard his boat. The weather today was ideal, and the prospect of spending time on the water certainly sounded appealing.

"What time should I be there?"

"I'll meet you in the Marina parking area at six o'clock," he answered. "We'll have a cocktail or two and dine fashionably late."

I had acted impulsively, and as I hung up, a flood of emotions ran through me – all mixed. I felt guilty as I thought of Ronny, but at the same time I was excited.

The offer seemed harmless enough, and after a year maybe it wouldn't hurt to spend a little time with a man I found attractive.

45

Staying up here in Sault Ste. Marie, I thought I'd left my problems with the mob miles behind. But a phone call that came from Detroit just five minutes later rocked my boat. The caller was Joe Sachs, a reporter who usually sat three desks from me back at the *Times*.

"Heard the one about the two hoodlums who walk into a bar looking for a reporter?"

"No."

"Well you should. The reporter they were looking for is you."

Sachs wondered why his humor often went unappreciated. He explained that two of the mob's finest showed up at *Thirty* asking questions about my whereabouts. I wasn't laughing.

"Pap Cohen told me all about it a little over an hour ago. I was eating a late lunch at the bar."

Pap Cohen was the owner and often bartender of *Thirty*, the tavern where many a *Times, News and Free Press* reporter drank the workday to a close. The joint got its name from the signature mark of -30- that reporters traditionally type after the last paragraph of copy to denote the end of a story.

I tried not to sound too alarmed. "What did Pap tell them?"

"Just that you were out of town on assignment; and no one seemed to know where."

That was probably accurate. "Who else besides you and Wells knows where I am?"

Sachs paused. "No one. Problem is: most people around here know your uncle is publisher of the Soo Morning News. Someone could slip in conversation and the hoods might put two and two together."

"I doubt Zerilli's boys are smart enough to add two and two," I said. "But let me know if they come poking around again. Keep your ears open."

"Speaking of ears, have you heard the one about the four-foot-tall hearing aid salesman who walks into a bar?"

"Goodbye Joe."

Sachs' call bothered me more than I let on. With nearly 300 miles between me and Detroit, I figured I'd be safe.

Now I wasn't so sure.

46

I pulled into the Riverbend Marina a shade after six o'clock and found Scotty standing beside his big black Packard in the gravel parking lot. He looked nautically suave in khaki slacks, a blue blazer and white deck shoes. I had on the same white blouse and black slacks I had worn earlier in the day, but had stopped by the house to feed Mick and pick up a pair of white tennis shoes.

I laced up the shoes, and as we walked across the gravel toward the river, I could see that there were no more than fifteen boats moored at a series of docks that could have held a hundred.

"It's the fuel shortage," Scotty said. "Most of the people who dock here never took their boats out of winter storage. Even the ones you see here probably haven't left the docks this season. Their owners visit on weekends, sleep on them overnight and spend the days sunbathing and partying around the marina."

The evening was gorgeous: temperature in the mid-seventies, with a refreshing breeze blowing in off the two-mile-wide St. Marys River. Seagulls flew overhead (not directly overhead, thank goodness), occasionally swooping down to the river to pluck a silvery snack from the surface. Most of the boats tied along the docks were cruisers, somewhere between twenty-five and fifty feet in length. But one beautiful white yacht stood out from the rest.

"That one has to be ninety feet long," I said, pointing to it.

"Ninety six," Scotty said. "C'mon, I'll show you."

We walked up the gangplank of the monstrous yacht and Scotty unfastened a chain he called the boarding gate and motioned me to follow him onto the deck.

"This is your boat?" It was a rhetorical question; Scotty had intimated that he was wealthy, but this yacht had to cost at least two hundred thousand dollars.

"Afraid so," Scotty said. "With fuel rationing on, the former owner couldn't afford enough diesel to run it across the river and back. He gave me a great price."

Scotty held a door open and I stepped into the main cabin. I'm not easily impressed by boats. Living near Grosse Pointe, Michigan, one of the country's most affluent communities, I had been aboard some of the finest yachts on Lake St. Clair. But the interior of this one was nothing short of magnificent. I found myself standing in the center of a living area most Grosse Pointers would have been proud to have in their homes.

"Welcome to the Caiman's main salon," said Scotty. I know my mouth must have been hanging open.

The floor was highly polished teak and the couches and chairs mirrored each other in the same brownish red shade of soft, rich leather. A fireplace graced one end of the cabin, a gleaming mahogany bar the other. There were windows all around, affording passengers a spectacular view of the river.

"Just a little touch of home," Scotty grinned.

"Wow!" I finally managed to say. "Some home!"

"C'mon, let me show you around." We paused at the bar toward the back of the salon, where Scotty poured a Scotch and water for me and a bourbon and water for himself. Then, glass in hand he led the way down a narrow staircase positioned just beside the bar.

Once below, we walked along a narrow hallway with staterooms on each side. We ended up at the open doorway to what was obviously the yacht's master stateroom. I leaned in and took in the view: a large double bed, covered with a rich, light blue comforter, polished wooden cabinets and a shining wood floor covered by a colorful oriental rug.

Was it my imagination or did Scotty hover there behind me a second too long? "Let's take a look at that back porch upstairs," I said quickly.

"Sure," Scotty said. "But if you're going to be a boater, you'll have to learn the terminology. It's not a back porch, it's the fantail."

We went up the stairs again to the main salon where Scotty opened the door to the fantail and we walked out onto it. The area resembled a large, covered porch, and ran some 25 feet from the rear of the main salon to the boat's stern. The deck was the same polished teak; the furniture, wicker couches and chairs, were covered with matching thick, blue patterned cushions.

In the center of it all was a white cloth-covered table set for two diners. Standing next to it was a smiling chef, holding a bottle of red wine.

It turned out to be just the beginning of the surprises in store this evening.

47

"I've imported Chef Joseph from the Park Place Hotel downstate in Traverse City," Scotty said. "He's going to chef a party I'm having aboard in two weeks. He's here today and tomorrow making preparations, so I talked him into creating a special meal just for us."

Scotty held my chair as I sat down. Chef Joseph poured a sample of wine into Scotty's glass, which he swirled around and then tasted.

"Cheval Blanc, 1934. Excellent choice, Joseph."

"Thank you, Sir."

"Pour a glass for Miss Brennan."

"Yes, Sir. I had the Cheval Blanc decanted on-shore for two hours to let it breathe. I did the same with the bottle of Croft Vintage Port, 1927, you'll enjoy after dinner along with a delicious cheese from Traverse City."

I couldn't help looking around as Chef Joseph poured the wine, taking in the fantail area. Except for six posts that ran from the three-foot railing to the ceiling, the fantail was open all around. The result was a great view of the St. Marys River where two giant freighters sounded their foghorns as they passed, traveling in opposite directions.

Chef Joseph made a big production of preparing our entire meal at the tableside. He began with a Caesar salad, grinding anchovies in the bottom of a large dish, and adding the other ingredients with a flourish. He was equally flamboyant with the main course, filet mignon. He began with crushed peppercorns, added a dash or two of wine to the pan and fried them tableside. He completed his performance with a desert of Bananas Foster and a snack of imported French cheese.

We chatted as we ate. "When you told me you owned a boat, I had no idea it would be anything like this," I said. "It was a real surprise."

Scotty took a sip of his Cheval Blanc. "I have another surprise. The Caiman is going to be the first boat through the new MacArthur Lock on the day of its dedication."

"You're joking."

"Nope. I volunteered the Caiman and the governor took me up on it. In fact, Governor Kelly himself will be aboard for the dedication, along with some Army brass, the Mayor and a bunch of state senators and other officials."

"Sounds like a big deal."

"I'm having a party on board two weeks from tomorrow night to celebrate. You're invited, along with everyone on the Morning News staff. I hope you'll plan to be here."

Scotty went on to describe how, during the dedication ceremony, the officials would make their speeches from the bow of the Caiman. And how afterward it would sail out of the MacArthur Lock into the St. Marys River, Whitefish Bay and then on into Lake Superior.

Darkness was setting in as we finished the meal. The fantail lights were low, providing a romantic atmosphere. Freighters slid by out on the River, their lights dancing in the darkness. A cool breeze cut through the warm summer air, and all seemed right with the world. It was a truly magical evening.

Chef Joseph had left us alone and we moved to a wicker couch next to the railing. We sat sipping from our wine glasses, looking out over the water. The trees, a mile or so across the river, were dark shapes. Sea gulls slipped through the evening air above us. I felt Scotty slip his arm around behind me. Maybe it was the wine, maybe the company, but it all felt very comfortable. I leaned back against Scotty's arm, looked up into his eyes and we kissed. It started off innocently enough, but became very sensual.

It was time to slow things down.

"Tell me about this shindig you're planning," I said.

Scotty pulled back a little as he answered. "Are you coming?"

"Of course I am."

"Swell. The governor and mayor will be here, along with some state senators, the sheriff and most of the brass from the Army Corps of Engineers."

"You must carry a lot of weight to pull people like that into your party," I said.

"Frankly, it's not me so much as the fact that if I find that vein of copper where I think it is, the Soo economy will boom. That always makes politicians look good. We're blasting every day. And every day we get a little closer to the mother lode."

Scotty leaned closer and again we kissed. Again it got more passionate. I broke off the kiss; there was something I needed to know before this relationship went any further.

"Scotty?"

"Yes, Kate?"

"Did you ever date Shirley Benoit?"

His eyebrows furrowed. "Why do you ask?"

"Shirley and I were having a girl-to-girl chat the evening before she . . . she was killed. She warned me to keep away from you. Why would she do that?"

Scotty looked relieved. "Oh, that," he said. "Yeah, Shirley and I went out a couple of times. We hit it off pretty well, but I'm afraid Shirley was getting too serious, too fast."

"So you . . ."

"I decided to call it off. I wasn't ready for that kind of commitment. And I'm afraid . . . well, Shirley never forgave me."

"I see."

"I was sorry to hurt her. I hoped someday she'd forgive me. As it turned out . . . well, that's impossible. It was a shame she was murdered like that."

"If it makes you feel any better, I don't think they hold grudges where Shirley is now," I said.

It was getting late. My watch showed it was nearly ten o'clock and I had to be at work the next morning. I stood up.

"It's been a lovely evening, Scotty. Thanks so much."

"I'm staying aboard the Caiman tonight," he said. "But I'll walk you to your car."

We kissed again in the parking lot before I started home.

48

Mick was waiting for me when I got home, patiently as usual. I let him out into the backyard, then sat down at the kitchen table and poured a glass of milk.

I was still reeling from the evening's events. Whether I wanted to admit it or not, I had let a man into my life. I hoped the decision wasn't one I'd regret. Scotty had been the perfect host from the beginning of the evening to the end, walking me to my car.

What would come next?

And what about beyond that? I was, after all, still a reporter for the *Detroit Times*. I looked forward to the time I could return and finish what I'd begun: the series on organized crime and their production of gasoline ration stamps in the Detroit area.

Suddenly I relaxed, realizing I was taking this all too seriously. I had gone from not wanting another man in my life under any circumstances to considering my plans for the future.

All in one short evening.

But what an evening! Scotty's Caiman was one fantastic yacht. It was so spectacular, in fact, that it was to be the first to sail through the new McArthur Lock.

Then it dawned on me: the reports of the threat of a German attack on the day of the dedication. Had Scotty been warned of it? The threat was supposedly top secret, but Scotty was obviously well connected. He might have been notified even before I found out.

I had been sworn to secrecy, but that was before tonight. I had to at least tell Scotty about the possibility of an attack, without revealing the source.

I'd tell him tomorrow. It was time now for some sleep.

Mick apparently agreed; he was scratching at the back door.

49

Friday, June 25

Olson's report seemed so one-sided I felt confident that Crawford would let me write the story of my interview with the Corporal.

So I decided to write it without asking.

I vowed to be as objective as I could, given that I was convinced of Cummins' innocence. I even called Sheriff Valenti to get his reaction to what I was writing.

"Cummins is the only suspect we have in custody at this time," was the best the sheriff could do. He gave no reaction at all to the coroner's view that the killer had to be right-handed. "Cummins is the only suspect we have in custody," he repeated.

I called the coroner and elicited a quote from him, underlining his right-handed killer theory.

Then I wrote the story.

It was minutes from deadline when I dropped the typewritten pages on Crawford's desk. He looked at the papers, looked up at me, and then back to the papers and began to read.

He looked up again when he finished. "You interviewed Cummins?"

"I did. He had been accused of killing my best friend," I said. "I had to find out, for Shirley's sake, if he did it."

"And you're convinced the sheriff has the wrong man?"

"The coroner says the killer was right-handed. Cummins writes with his left hand. Besides, I've interviewed more real killers than I care to admit. And Cummins just isn't the type."

"If we run your story, won't it appear that we're contradicting ourselves?"

"Look, Mr. Crawford ..."

"Call me Jack."

"Jack. Suppose Cummins is innocent. Suppose Sheriff Valenti catches the real killer. How will the newspaper look if we've only run Olson's story? A story that practically condemns Cummins without a trial."

Crawford mulled that over. "Alright," he said finally. "But I want you to strike one sentence."

"What sentence is that?" *As if I didn't know.*

"The sentence about Sheriff Valenti not knowing his right hand from his left."

"You got it, Jack!"

50

Mick was excited to see me when I got home that evening.

He stood on his one hind leg, his paws on top of the fence gate, wagging his tail and barking madly.

I patted his head, then went through the gate and around to the back door of the house with Mick following, still barking.

It seemed as if he were trying to tell me something.

I went in through the unlocked back door and walked to the cupboard where I kept Mick's dry dog food. Maybe he was hungry. I poured a larger than usual helping of dry food into his bowl and set it on the floor next to the refrigerator.

Mick took a look at the bowl, barked a couple more times and then began to eat. I walked through the kitchen, into the dining room.

That's when I noticed the flower vase. There had been a small chip on the lip of the vase and I distinctly remembered turning that side toward the wall so visitors wouldn't notice it. Now it faced the opposite way, where it could be easily seen from anywhere in the room.

Was I going nuts? I didn't think so. I decided to look around.

Things got a bit unsettling as I began to explore the rest of the first floor. There was a strange feeling that, somehow, drawers and closets had been searched through and then had their items returned – almost to the original places.

Almost.

Most people wouldn't have noticed, but my years as a reporter had trained me to focus on small details. My career depended on it.

If I believed in poltergeists, I'd figure that Shirley had been here, moving things around just to say hello. I didn't believe in ghosts, of course, but I still found the placement of the items unsettling.

Someone had searched Shirley's house while I was at the office. What had he, she or they been looking for?

A chill ran through me with my next thought – were they still in the house? I held my breath – listening.

Hearing nothing, I decided to search further. Mick had finished eating and I took him with me as I went down to the basement. I opened closets and drawers, finding the same conditions as on the first floor. Small details no one else would have seen gave away the fact that the basement had been gone over one end to the other.

Then I tried the attic. I hit the light switch at the bottom of the stairway and went up, Mick close behind. I reached the top of the stairs and looked around the attic. The unfinished walls were bare two-by-four planks with insulation affixed between them. Light emanated from a lone bulb hanging from the ceiling. My suitcases lay where I had left them, against the wall next to an old set of golf clubs. A cardboard box in the far corner intrigued me and I walked over to it.

Opening the lid, I could see the box contained notebooks and papers and I slid it out in the open so I could inspect the contents under the light of the single bulb.

Shirley's high school yearbook was inside, along with a notebook containing the names and what appeared to be the current addresses of some of our old school friends. There were five diaries in the box, one from each of her four high school years, and one from her freshman year in college.

I picked up the diary of her senior year in high school and scanned it. Page by page Shirley had kept details of her activities, complete with names and dates. My name appeared often and brought back memories that caused my eyes to tear.

I replaced the diaries in the box. I hadn't wanted to invade Shirley's privacy, but felt it necessary to find what was here. I learned she was very meticulous in her note keeping.

I walked back downstairs mulling the questions. The fact that the house had been searched made me feel as if I'd been violated. Everything I touched seemed to bear some sort of stigma.

I made a hasty search of Shirley's room and then my own. I noticed that a couple of dollar bills and a few coins I had placed on the dresser in my bedroom last evening were still there. The motive for the search had obviously not been robbery.

As I walked back into the living room, I considered calling the sheriff, then thought better of it. What would I report? That a chip on the lip of a vase had been turned away from the wall? That I suspected someone had gone through the house, but nothing was missing?

I opened a can of vegetable soup and fixed a salad of lettuce, a couple of carrots and a couple slices of fresh tomato. Bedtime came shortly after nine-thirty. The next day would be an eventful one.

Tomorrow was Shirley's funeral.

51

Claus Krueger viewed the upcoming operation scheduled for the dedication of the new lock as any good soldier would.

He felt no animosity toward the American people; on the contrary, his father had instilled a respect for the Americans in him at an early age. The fact that hundreds of innocent people would die was a necessary adjunct of the war.

Krueger considered the purpose behind the operation a stroke of genious. The German high command had always suspected that the Americans were soft; the current generation had never felt the pain of war on their native soil as the people of Germany had. More than four hundred thousand German civilians had been killed during the World War of twenty-five years ago.

The attack on the locks and the resulting slaughter of civilians would finally bring the sting of battle home to U.S. soil. Once Americans realized the true cost – that war was more than marching bands and waving flags - they would have no stomach for it. They would rush to convince their congressmen and even the President himself, to put an end to this "senseless conflict".

Roosevelt would be forced to pull American troops out of Europe and the Pacific, leaving the Third Reich free to continue its blitzkrieg across Europe, while the Japanese took the Pacific.

The operation now lay just days away and he, Claus Krueger, would play a major role. The more Americans that died, the quicker their countrymen would capitulate. And the more impressive his welcome would be upon his return to the Fatherland.

He wasn't inhumane. He wasn't a monster.

He was simply a good soldier.

52

Saturday, June 26

Shirley's funeral turned out to be the tearjerker I had anticipated.

The casket sat in a room just outside the chapel of Rodger's Funeral Home. A crowd had formed and people talked in hushed tones. Girls who had worked with Shirley at Blades Larue's stood around crying and hugging.

There's nothing like a funeral to remind people of how precious and fragile life is, and how petty their day-to-day disagreements can be. People who may have been involved in vehement arguments the day before now embraced.

I had never seen Blades Larue in anything other than an open collared shirt before and apparently he hadn't either. The narrow end of his blue and white striped tie hung three inches below the wide one. His baggy sport coat hung on him like a bed sheet. I could tell by the redness of his eyes that Shirley's death had had a profound effect on him.

Blades had closed for the morning, and his entire crew was in attendance. I recognized Mrs. Miller's daughter Felice even though I hadn't seen her since she was in junior high. I waved, making a mental note to say hello to her after the funeral service.

I finally worked up enough nerve to approach Shirley's casket. I said a silent prayer and turned away.

G.P., Andy Checkle and Carol Olson stood in a corner near the door to the chapel and I walked over to join them. I hugged G.P., who expressed his condolences to me as if Shirley had been my sister, which she nearly was. I hugged Andy, whose face turned a bright shade of red nearly matching his hair. I reached out my hand to Olson, who took it.

Just as we started to speak, a dark suited employee of the funeral parlor made an announcement and people began moving into the chapel. The lid was closed over Shirley and several young men grabbed the casket by the handles and carried it in, setting it carefully in front of a small altar covered with flowers.

An organist played softly as the four of us sat near the rear of the room: Olson, G.P. and Andy in the chair next to me. Andy leaned over and whispered to me. "I feel awkward, Kate. I've only been to one other funeral, my grandfather's. And I was just a kid then."

I patted Andy on the knee. "You're not alone, Andy. Funerals are always tough."

Especially when it's your best friend lying in the casket. I couldn't help seeing Shirley's laughing face in my mind. We had had such fun just two nights ago. She had been so alive. I dabbed at my eyes with a tissue I pulled from my purse.

The chapel was filling up. It seemed half the town was there. Shirley had many friends from our days in high school, and she had made more since moving back last January. I noticed a couple who looked to be in their fifties sitting in the front row. I had never seen them before and wondered if they might be Shirley's relatives. I knew she had an uncle and aunt living somewhere in the Upper Peninsula.

Just as the organist was finishing the prelude, Jack Crawford came in and sat in the empty chair beside me. He smiled and, surprisingly, reached over and squeezed my hand.

You could have knocked me over with a hymnal.

I heard quiet voices behind us and turned around to see Scotty Banyon enter the chapel. He took a seat in the last row.

The service itself went by fairly quickly. The young pastor of the Presbyterian Church Shirley had attended officiated. In his eulogy he remarked how Shirley had made it to Sunday morning services even when she had worked until closing at Blades' restaurant the night before. He drew a laugh from the crowd when he good-naturedly mentioned that Shirley hadn't always been able to stay awake during his sermons.

Rock of Ages, one of Shirley's favorite hymns concluded the service and we walked out into the lobby. Shirley would be buried later, so there would be no procession to the cemetery.

Scotty came over to join our group. He shook hands with the men and smiled at Carol Olson. He leaned over and gave me a peck on the cheek before apologizing that he had to get back to his work. Given what he had told me about his relationship with Shirley, he might have felt awkward about being there.

After Scotty left, I tried to locate the couple I had spotted in the front row, with no luck. They had apparently left via a side door immediately after the service. But just as I started to leave, Mrs. Miller's daughter Felice caught up with me.

"I thought that was you, Felice," I said. "You've changed a bit since Junior High."

"You haven't changed at all," she said. "Mother said she saw you the other evening. I wonder . . . could we talk outside?"

What was this about? "Sure. Let's go."

We stood in the parking lot, Felice waiting until most of the crowd had filed past us on the way to their cars before speaking.

"I read the story about your interview with Corporal Cummins," she said finally. "You really believe he's innocent?"

"I do. I'm convinced he just happened to be in the wrong place at the wrong time."

"If I tell you something, will you promise not to write it or even talk about it to anyone?"

"I'm a reporter, Felice. I never reveal my sources when they want to remain anonymous."

"I don't mean that," she said. "I mean you can't write about what I tell you. Or tell anyone else about it."

"In journalism we call that background. It may be the foundation under a story, but it's not reported per se. Is that what you mean?"

Her lips pursed. "I guess so."

"Okay, what is it?"

"Corporal Cummins couldn't have killed Shirley," Felice said. "When Shirley was murdered . . ." Felice paused, looking down at the pavement.

"Yes?"

"Roy was with me."

53

Felice's words caught me by surprise.

"You were with Corporal Cummins?"

"Roy and I were seeing each other. We'd go for walks and talk. We seemed to have so much in common."

I nodded, urging her to continue.

"He had been a teacher before he went into the Army. That's what I want to do. I'm trying to save money for college.

"He was so caring, so willing to help others. He could have made a lot more money coming back home to Michigan to teach. But he stayed in Louisiana, knowing the people there needed him more."

"Were you in love?"

Felice paused again. "I can't speak for Roy," she said finally. "But I know how I felt about him, and . . ."She choked back a tear. "Yes, I was falling in love with Roy. And now he's in jail. It isn't fair. He wouldn't hurt a soul. And he couldn't have killed Shirley. He was with me."

"Tell me about that evening."

Felice couldn't have been more than nine or ten when I last saw her. I had graduated from Sault Ste. Marie High School and moved back to Detroit. She had to be at least 20 now, and had a presence beyond her physical age.

"We always went for our walks in the same place," she said. "Along the beach two miles or so west of town. We'd take off our shoes and walk in the sand. We knew we'd be alone."She added quickly, "We had to be, of course."

"And that night?"

"It was right after the riot started downstate. The fighting between races affected Roy terribly. It was spreading to his old neighborhood and he knew it wouldn't be long before his friends and family would be involved."

She pulled a handkerchief from her purse and wiped her eyes. "We hadn't walked very far when Roy stopped. Just stopped. I asked him what was bothering him." Felice stopped talking as three people walked by us on the way to their cars. We both nodded a greeting to them.

"What did he say?" I asked.

"Roy said he thought we were being foolish. The riot had convinced him we were living a fairy tale; and that fairy tales don't work in the real world."

There was more silence as Felice wiped her eyes. "And then he walked away from me. I tried to follow, but he shooed me away. I got in my car and caught up to him; tried to convince him to get in . . . to come back to town with me.

"But Roy just kept walking. He went down farther toward the water where I couldn't follow."

"So you drove back home?"

Felice nodded. "And the deputies must have picked him up a short time afterwards." She began to sob. I reached my arm around her, trying to comfort her. A couple walked by us, staring, but kept on going.

Felice finally looked up at me. "Have you ever loved someone you found you couldn't have, Kate?"

Ronny! It was my turn to pause. "Yes. Yes, I have Felice. I know exactly what you're going through."

"Is there any way you could get a note to Roy for me? I mean, can you get into the jail to see him?"

"I guess I could ask for another interview. But I can't guarantee anything."

That answer was good enough. Felice took a pencil and small slip of paper from her purse and spent the next few minutes writing. Finished, she folded the paper and handed it to me.

"Please don't read it," she said. "I'd be very embarrassed."

"What you wrote is between you and Roy," I said. "I wouldn't dream of reading it."

I turned to walk to my car when Felice called after me.

"Kate, do you think it will ever be possible for us all to get along? I mean white and colored. To live together?"

I stopped and turned back to her.

"I hope so, Felice. I really do."

54

Sunday, June 27

Funerals have a way of making you appreciate just being alive.

The next day I attended services at the tiny Presbyterian Church where Shirley had been a member since our high school days. The minister, who had conducted Shirley's funeral service the day before, delivered the sermon. He mentioned Shirley's name several times, reciting how she would be missed and repeating how often she attended church despite working late hours the night before.

Afterwards it was time to see if I could talk my way into the Sault Ste. Marie jail for a visit with Roy Cummins.

It turned out to be much easier than I thought. The deputy at the front desk, while in his fifties, seemed to be new at this job. He gave my credentials a cursory look, accompanied me back to Cummins' cell, and left me with the corporal.

"I don't have anything more to tell you," Cummins said when we were alone. He stood at the cell door, his forearms resting on the bar.

"I have something to tell you," I said. I spoke quietly to avoid eavesdropping from the white prisoners in the cell to the left, or the colored prisoners just beyond them. "I had a conversation yesterday with Felice Miller."

The news startled Cummins. He had been gazing at the floor. Now he looked up; I had his full attention.

"I know why you couldn't possibly have stabbed Shirley Benoit."

"You can't use that," he said.

"You're facing a murder charge. Michigan doesn't have the death penalty, but you could spend the rest of your life in prison."

"I'll deny everything. I won't involve Felice in this."

"She's your only alibi."

"Then I'll have to depend on my attorney. The Army is providing one."

"I hope he's good," I said. "He'll have to be."

Corporal Cummins was bull-headed, to be sure. But I left the jailhouse with more determination than ever to help prove his innocence.

55

At 1600 hours that Sunday afternoon Claus Krueger walked to the closet in his bedroom and retrieved a trunk hidden back against the wall.

He reached inside the trunk and carefully removed the Enigma machine. Closing the lid, he placed the coding machine on top.

The Wehrmacht Enigma consisted of a combination of mechanical and electrical systems working together. The mechanical mechanism included a keyboard and a set of rotating discs known as rotors. The rotors enabled the Enigma to vary the substitution of letters, making the decoding of an intercepted message extremely difficult. Sometimes the letter C would be substituted by the letter N, for instance, other times it was M or X. The machine receiving the message would decode it automatically.

Krueger turned on the Enigma and it began typing out a message almost immediately.

Bestaetigen Sie: Operation Todschlag, punkt 1500 Uhr.11.Juli. *Verify Operation Deathstrike set for 1500 hours, July 11.*

Krueger typed his answer: Bestaetigt. *Verified.*

He then asked a question to assure himself of safe passage back to the Fatherland via U-boat once the mission was accomplished: Bestaetigen Sie termin am Treffpunkt, 0500 Uhr, 13.Juli. *Verify rendezvous at checkpoint, 500 hours, July 13.*

Momentarily the machine replied: Bestaetigt. Aber zeit fenster ist knapp, Sie haben nur 20 minuten. *Verified. But the window of time is short. You will have only 20 minutes.*

Krueger replied: Verstanden.

He waited a few minutes for further messages. Satisfied there were none, he closed the machine and placed it back in the trunk.

Despite the Enigma code, each transmission bore a certain amount of risk and there would be no further communication unless something went terribly wrong.

The mission was on.

56

Monday, June 28

I had spent the weekend mulling over the events of the last two days.

Felice's confession confirmed what I had felt all along. Corporal Roy Cummins had nothing to do with Shirley's death. The Sault Ste. Marie jail held an innocent man, and I was the only one besides Felice and Corporal Cummins who knew the real story. I had to convince authorities of Cummins' innocence without exposing the fact that he and Mrs. Miller's daughter had been together that evening.

But who had murdered Shirley? And why? It seemed obvious, at least to me, that her death was no random killing. The perpetrator had left Shirley's purse behind containing $21, a week's pay.

Whoever attacked her wanted her dead for some reason. I couldn't help feeling the key to finding out who murdered Shirley lay in discovering why she was killed.

By the time I reached the office Monday morning, I had decided to take my suspicions to Jack Crawford. But it turned out I might as well have been whistling *Dixie*. Or maybe Tommy Dorsey's new tune, *Sing, Sing, Sing.*

"Leave it alone, Kate," Crawford said. "Sheriff Valenti is convinced that they have the right man. His opinion is good enough for me and it ought to be good enough for you."

"The coroner says Shirley's murderer was right handed," I reminded him. "Corporal Cummins is left handed."

"Right handed, left handed, what difference does it make? Maybe he grabbed her with his left hand and stabbed her with the right. How do you know?"

"What difference does it make? It makes a hell of a lot of difference to an innocent man locked up in the jail for a murder he had nothing to do with."

"That's a job for the sheriff and the courts. Your job is reporting. And you turned in an excellent job on that interview with the corporal."

"Thanks. But I'm still determined to prove Corporal Cummins is innocent."

"How are you going to do that?"

"By finding the real killer."

"That's fine," Crawford said, "as long as you don't do it on the newspaper's time. I want you covering the progress of the new lock."

"I thought that was Andy's territory."

"It is, but with the dedication getting closer, I want you both on the assignment."

I'd wanted to cover the story of the new lock all along. But I left Crawford's office with the sneaking suspicion he was offering the assignment to keep me too busy to investigate Shirley's murder.

57

It was nearly five o'clock when I finally had time to myself and get back to my thoughts of finding Shirley's real killer.

Shirley and I had parted company right after high school. She enrolled at the University of Michigan, while I traveled east to the Columbia University School of Journalism. We ran into each other on occasional visits back home, but for the most part had gone our separate ways. During our last conversation together a few days ago, Shirley had mentioned dropping out of the U of M during her sophomore year in Ann Arbor.

That's where my investigation into her death would begin.

I called Sam Murphy, an old friend and colleague of mine at the *Times*. As the newspaper's Education Editor I knew he had good contacts at most of the major universities. After we exchanged a few pleasantries I got to the point.

"I'm going into the background of a woman who was murdered here at the Soo," I said. "Can you use your contacts to see if there is a record of where she went after she dropped out of the U of M?"

"I can try," Sam said. "Give me the dates she attended classes there."

I told Sam we had graduated from Soo High together in 1928, and she would have enrolled in the fall of that year. If she dropped out of college during her sophomore year, that would have been '29 or '30. He told me he'd check with his sources at the University and call me back.

What he found shocked me.

58

Tuesday, June 29

Sam Murphy got back to me just after lunch the next day. I took the call at my desk.

"Shirley Benoit graduated from the University of Michigan with high honors in the spring of 1932," Murphy reported. "Her major was accounting."

Graduated with high honors? During our conversation, Shirley told me she dropped out of college. *Why would she have made up a story like that?*

"You got me," Murphy said. "But I know my information is correct. It came right from the registrar's office. I just got off the phone with a woman I know who works there."

"Is there anyone there who might know where she went after she graduated?" I asked.

"I seriously doubt it," Murphy said. "Remember there were some ten thousand students at the University of Michigan when your friend Shirley left the Ann Arbor campus. With that many people they just can't make a rule of following each one after graduation."

"What about a counselor?" I asked.

"You could try. The name of her counselor would be on her records at the registrar's office."

Five minutes later I was on the phone to Shirley's counselor, a Mr. Tyson.

"I'm sorry," Tyson said. "There's nothing on Miss Benoit's transcript that indicates any type of job placement after she left the University. We do have a placement center, though. You could try there."

I did.

Dead end.

59

Wednesday, June 30

My investigation into Shirley's murder had run up against the proverbial brick wall.

I was disappointed; but I felt even worse about not being able to help prove that Corporal Cummins was innocent. He seemed willing to face a life sentence in prison rather than call on Felice as the only person who could convince a jury that he hadn't killed Shirley Benoit.

That's when the idea of a second option struck me. Maybe the weight of the *Soo Morning News* could be directed at the sheriff through its news and editorial pages.

I didn't know how much support I could get from Crawford, but it was worth a try. And I was willing to go over his head to my uncle if I had to.

Fortunately, I found both men in G.P.'s office the next morning. Without mentioning Felice's name, I laid out the story as I now knew it: that an unnamed source had confided that she had been with the corporal at the time of Shirley's murder. I ended my comments with a suggestion that the *Soo Morning News* champion the corporal's cause.

"I'm against it," Jack Crawford said almost before I had finished. "It's too risky right now. The whole damn situation could blow up right in our faces."

I wasn't going to let go that easily. "What do you mean, risky?"

"Don't you know what's going on downstate?" Crawford said. "Detroit is still recovering from a race riot that left the city practically in flames."

"But what's that got to do with Corporal Cummins?" I asked. "This is Sault Ste. Marie, not Detroit. And an innocent man is being held in jail."

G.P. weighed in. "There's some history you need to know about, Kate," he said. "When the army announced that troops would be sent up here to guard the locks, the townspeople were ecstatic. Most of our local boys are in the service, many serving in the artillery. The natural assumption was that they would be coming home."

"Yes?"

"Instead, the army sent a battalion of soldiers from New Orleans, most of them colored."

"How does that justify holding an innocent man in jail?"

Crawford frowned. "If Cummins is released now, it could rub the townspeople the wrong way. There could be trouble. Maybe a race riot right here."

I turned to my uncle. "G.P., you've always stood for what's right, no matter what the circumstances were. And right now the circumstance is that an innocent man is in jail."

He paused, his lips pursed. "Maybe there's a way to do the right thing, and still keep the peace among the townspeople."

"What do you mean?" asked Crawford.

"Kate, I want you to write an editorial. But don't go so far as suggesting Corporal Cummins' outright release. Instead, let's suggest he be turned over to his superiors at Fort Brady. I know Colonel Woods, the Fort Commander, and he's an honorable man. He'll hold the corporal accountable, but if he feels Cummins is as innocent as you do, he'll do the right thing."

Crawford started to object, but G.P. cut him off with a wave of his hand. "I understand the risks, Jack. But the Soo Morning News has a tradition of taking a strong position on human rights issues like this. We're not going to play dead on this, no matter what the repercussions might be."

I could have hugged my uncle, but thought better of it. I couldn't help smiling, though.

G.P. looked my way. "Kate get busy on that editorial. And I want you to write any follow up stories that might be needed."

My smile got brighter. "Thanks, G.P."

"That's on top of your assignment to cover the progress of the new lock."

"Yes, sir!"

I left the office in a hurry, already writing the editorial in my head.

60

Thursday, July 1, 1943

A Soo Morning News Editorial:
Our Jail Holds An Innocent Man

The people of Sault Ste. Marie are all too familiar with the tragic murder of Shirley Benoit, one of our town's most popular citizens. The young woman, who worked as a waitress at Blades Larue's Restaurant, was struck down by a ruthless killer last Thursday morning.

But there is a second tragedy that has risen out of Miss Benoit's murder of which we believe our town's residents should be aware. It is the arrest and incarceration of U.S. Army Corporal Roy Cummins. Corporal Cummins has been charged with Miss Benoit's murder.

The Soo Morning News believes that Corporal Cummins, a Negro, is guilty of nothing more than being in the wrong place at the wrong time. He was arrested by sheriff's deputies later that same morning two blocks from Blades Larue's Restaurant.

Miss Benoit was slashed with a sharp blade, causing a great loss of blood. Yet, when apprehended a short time later, Corporal Cummins had no blood on his hands or clothing.

Dr. Kenneth Larsen, Sault Ste. Marie's coroner for the past 20 years, states that the wounds on Miss Benoit's body point to a right-handed assailant. Corporal Cummins is left-handed.

The Soo Morning News believes strongly that Corporal Cummins is being held in our city's jail simply because Sheriff Carl Valenti lacks any other suspects in the case.

Further, it is our opinion that Sheriff Valenti should either show that he has more evidence of Corporal Cummins' guilt than he has produced so far, or turn the soldier over to the army at Fort Brady immediately.

61

Thursday, July 1
10 days before the dedication

I had expected a reaction from my editorial, but what happened surprised even me.

"You missed all the fireworks," Andy Checkle said as I arrived around ten o'clock Thursday morning. I had stopped at the Army Corps of Engineers to check on the progress of the MacArthur Lock.

"What are you talking about?" I asked.

Sheriff Valenti paid Crawford a visit early this morning," Andy said. "I'm surprised you didn't hear the shouting way over at the locks."

"Fill me in."

"Valenti wanted to know who wrote the editorial. Crawford stonewalled at first, saying whatever appears on the editorial page is the opinion of the entire Soo Morning News editorial staff. He told Valenti to forget it. He said it didn't matter who the individual writer was."

I wondered how long that lasted. I wondered how long Crawford kept it up before he caved in and told the sheriff I had written the opinion piece.

"So he finally broke down and told Valenti who wrote the editorial?" I asked.

"Yeah."

I shook my head. It was just a matter of time before the sheriff came looking for me.

"Crawford admitted that he wrote it," Andy said. "And then dared Valenti to do something about it."

Crawford? *Jack* Crawford? The same Jack Crawford I had been on the verge of telling to go to hell more times than I could count? *That* Jack Crawford?

"Yeah, Crawford really stood up to Valenti," Andy said. "Of course Valenti couldn't really do anything about it. Legally, I mean. But I wouldn't want to be in Crawford's shoes driving around town. Valenti will have his deputies on the alert. Why, as little as a mile an hour over the speed limit and Crawford will probably find himself paying a ticket."

"You're probably right," I said.

"Why would he write that editorial anyway?" Andy asked.

"What do you mean?"

"I thought Crawford was a smart guy. Why would he put his neck in a noose like that?"

"Maybe because he stood up for what he believed in," I said. I turned on my heel and walked to Crawford's office.

He was at his desk.

"Jack?"

He looked up.

"Thanks for sticking up for me."

He looked puzzled. "What do you mean?"

"Andy Checkle described your bout with Sheriff Valenti."

Crawford smiled. "I'm afraid that bout wasn't much more than a two rounder," he said. "Our good sheriff is a lot more bark than bite."

"Still, I appreciate it. And I'm sure Corporal Cummins would, too."

"Speaking of the corporal, I talked to his commanding officer, Colonel Woods."

"Yes?"

"The army's stepping in. They're going to demand custody of the corporal. And I think once they see the evidence, or lack of it, he's going to be a free man."

I found Andy Checkle waiting for me just outside Crawford's office.

"Say, about that editorial. . ."

"Yes?"

"Why. . .uh. . .you. . .you didn't. . ."

"Yes I did."

I left Andy scratching his head.

62

Friday, July 2

Finding G.P. alone in his office the next morning, I inquired whether the Canadian authorities had reported spotting anything suspicious during their air searches of northern Canada.

If the Germans were planning an air raid on the locks, their operations wouldn't have to be large, just big enough to assemble a few planes brought in by submarine in pieces. That and a strip long enough to take off.

"Sorry," G.P. said. "There's nothing so far. But I'm talking to my contacts in Washington every day. They can't say anything directly, of course. But I do get the impression that the British are still intercepting reports of an attempt on the locks during the dedication."

"What about calling off the ceremony?" I asked. "Has anyone considered the fact that thousands of lives will be at risk?"

"Of course they have, Kate," G.P. said. "You've seen the precautions the army is taking. They've set up four radar sites over in Ontario and places like Cochrane and Hearst. They'll give us an early warning, should the Nazis try anything. And with all those barrage balloons blocking the way, it would be darned near impossible for a plane to get within a half mile of the locks."

"And if one should?"

"The artillery will be waiting. I've talked with some of the soldiers manning those weapons. They're actually hoping the Krauts make it through. They're ready to blast them out of the sky."

I felt a little better after talking with G.P. He seemed convinced an attack couldn't possibly be successful.

Still, I couldn't get the picture out of my mind: thousands of innocent men, women and children being strafed by German dive bombers.

Later that afternoon, I got what I considered a fairly bright idea.

My investigation into Shirley's history had run into a dead end in Ann Arbor. Maybe I could find out more about Shirley by starting here in the Soo and tracking backwards. It was a long shot, but I had nothing else to go on. I decided to pay a visit to Blades Larue.

63

It was mid-afternoon when I reached Blades Larue's and with the lunch rush over, I found the place nearly empty. I saw Felice Miller back in the kitchen and waved to her. She came out to greet me.

"Kate, I want to thank you for all you did to get Roy freed," she said.

"He's not being held anymore?"

"When the sheriff turned him over to the army, Roy's commanding officer took one look at the so-called evidence and told him to report back to duty. He's manning one of the guns at the locks right now."

I glanced around the room at the few occupants. No one was listening to our conversation. "What's in the future for you two?"

She looked down at the floor. "We've decided to go separate ways," she said. "Roy was right. After the war he's going back to the South to teach. He knows he's needed there. And . . ." She paused. "There's no future for what they call a mixed marriage."

Blades Larue walked in the back door from the alley. "Hi, Kate," he called. "You here for an early supper?"

I told Blades what I was looking for: any references Shirley might have provided when he hired her last January.

"Let me look," he said. "Seems to me she had worked at a restaurant over toward Wisconsin."

I said goodbye to Felice and followed Blades back through the kitchen, into his small office. Papers were scattered everywhere. They littered the top of his wooden desk. He sat in the chair after clearing a pile of papers from it and reached down into the bottom drawer of the desk.

He retrieved another pile of papers and began to leaf through them. This was obviously a routine he went through often. "Pay dirt," he said triumphantly, holding up one sheet. "Shirley worked at a place called The Stop Inn over in Negaunee. Owned by a Mr. and Mrs. Wilson."

"Is there a telephone number?"

"Sure. Call from here if you'd like."

Blades must have been feeling generous; it was a long distance call. I made it a point to place it station-to-station so it wouldn't cost as much.

"Hello?" It was a woman's voice.

"Mrs. Wilson?"

"Yes."

"Mrs. Wilson, I'm calling about a woman who worked for you up until last December. Her name was Shirley Benoit."

There was silence at the other end of the line.

"Mrs. Wilson? Mrs. Wilson, are you there?"

"Yes. But I don't know any Shirley Benoit. I'm sorry." There was a click on the other end of the line and she was gone.

64

I got back to the *Morning News* just in time to find Jack Crawford leaving for the day.

"Jack, can I see you for a minute?"

He did an about face and walked back into his office. I followed and closed the door.

He turned to face me. "What's this all about?"

"I need a couple of days off."

"Days off? With the July 4th weekend and Wednesday's special historical edition coming up? You've got to be kidding."

"Jack, I may have found a clue to Shirley's murder." I went through my findings with Crawford, ending with the call to the woman at the Stop Inn. "So you see, I've got to go to Negaunee."

"Look Kate, you're a reporter not a private detective. Leave these matters to the professionals. The sheriff, for instance."

"Professionals? You mean the sheriff who locked up the wrong man? The sheriff who kept him in jail for days even though it was probable that he was innocent?

"That's the professional you want me to trust with finding the murderer of my best friend?"

Crawford headed toward the door. "Kate with the dedication coming up I need you here at the Morning News. And I need you every day. That's final."

With that, he walked out and closed the door, leaving me in his office.

I ran to the door, but when I opened it, Crawford was already heading down the steps and out the front door.

65

Saturday, July 3

I woke up the next morning looking forward to my single day off. With the dedication near, we were all expected to work through the following week and weekend. But I vowed I would celebrate my freedom today.

The radio had the latest news from Europe: RAF bombers had raided Trapani, Sicily and Olbia, Sardinia.

I had just finished dressing when I heard a knock at the front door.

I was surprised to see Jack Crawford standing on the porch. "I, uh, I just came over to talk for a minute," he said. It was the first time I had ever seen him fumbling for words.

"Come in, Mr. Crawford." It was back to "Mr. Crawford." I still felt miffed from his attitude the day before.

I invited him to sit on the couch in the front room; I took one of the two overstuffed chairs. As we sat, Mick entered the room, and to my surprise, walked over to Crawford and hopped up on the couch next to him as if they were old friends.

Traitor!

Crawford placed a hand on Mick's head and began scratching him behind the ears. Again, I found myself amazed at the size of his paws – Crawford's not Mick's. His hand covered Mick's huge head like a yarmulke.

For his part, Mick seemed to relish the attention, closing his eyes and soaking it all in.

"I'm sorry if I seemed a bit gruff last evening," Crawford began. "It was a tough day at the office and I'm afraid I took it out on you."

He looked at me as if he expected some sort of commiseration, but damned if I was going to give him any quarter.

He went on. "You really want to carry out this investigation of yours?"

"Shirley Benoit was a special friend," I said. "I think I owe her memory the courtesy of finding out why she died, and if possible, who killed her."

"And you think that necessitates taking time off for a drive to Negaunee?"

I went back over what I had told him the evening before. "Mrs. Wilson, the woman who owns the Stop Inn, the restaurant where Shirley claimed she worked, says she never heard of her," I said. "That just doesn't' wash. Shirley's not the type who would falsify her resume."

Crawford nodded, his lips pursed. "Alright, I'll give you three days off."

I suddenly felt much better about Crawford. Maybe Mick had him pegged right after all. "Thank you, Jack. I won't let you or the newspaper down. I know there's a story here."

He held up a hand. "But, there's a condition. This is the Independence Day weekend and I need your help. I also need you on the Lock History Edition due out Wednesday. If you'll work from today through Monday, I'll give you the next three days off immediately afterwards."

It was better than nothing.

"You've got a deal."

66

Sunday, July 4

With Independence Day falling on a Sunday this year, Congress decreed the holiday would be observed on the following Monday. For the people of Sault Ste. Marie it turned out to be a two-day holiday.

Our country's birthday, always a big deal, was an even more important event in wartime, and the town fathers decided to go all out in a celebration that stretched over both days.

The faithful attended church on Sunday morning; then most headed for one of the many parks around town. Softball and volleyball games were in full swing by two o'clock.

Unfortunately, I wasn't among the celebrants. I had agreed to work both Sunday and Monday and as a result, I divided my time scouting around town for stories, and writing them up back at the office.

The wire services reported that a huge force of RAF heavy bombers had raided the Kalk and Deutz industrial districts near Cologne. The Brits were making inroads into Germany's industrial areas. Meanwhile, Allied bombers attacked Axis airfields in Sicily.

Late Sunday evening I found myself at the new MacArthur Lock. I talked to the Army captain in charge of overseeing the construction crew, who assured me the work would be completed before next Sunday, the day of the official dedication. The lock had been built in an incredibly short time by crews working around the clock.

Darkness was starting to settle in and I had decided to head for home when I noticed the familiar face of a man standing next to an anti-aircraft gun pointed out toward Whitefish Bay at the end of the new lock.

67

"Hello, Miss Brennan. Looking for a story?"

I greeted Corporal Roy Cummins with a smile. "Just checking on preparations for tomorrow, corporal," I said. "Good to see you're back."

Corporal Cummins returned the smile. "The colonel took one look at the evidence and chased me out of his office. Told me to get my tail back to work."

"So you're free and clear."

"Not exactly. There's a hearing coming up a week from this Wednesday. But my captain says it's just a formality as long as I 'keep my nose clean;' which I definitely plan to do."

I pointed to the ancient-looking anti-aircraft gun he was manning. "Are you sure that thing's powerful enough to bring down a Nazi dive bomber?"

He put a hand on the weapon. "Old Betsy may not be the latest government issue, but she'll do just fine."

He introduced me to the soldier with him, a Private Johnson. "He feeds Betsy here," Cummins said, pointing to a clip of ammunition beside the carriage. "And I fire."

The barrel of the weapon, a slender two inches in diameter, couldn't have been more than eight feet in length. It was mounted on a small carriage that had two large spoke wheels in front, two smaller ones in the back. It was a far cry from the anti-aircraft artillery I had seen in photographs from England.

"It looks like a holdover from the last war," I said.

Cummins smiled sheepishly. "More like the Second Boer War," he said. "The Boers used guns like this against the British. The Brits were impressed and adopted the design for themselves. This one was made by Vickers. The Army bought them from the British before this war started."

I looked at the gun skeptically. "Will it bring down a plane?"

"Don't worry, she'll do just fine," Cummins said. Then he spoke as if he were reciting from an Army manual: "She fires a one-pound shell accurately up to 3,000 feet vertically, 5,000 feet horizontally. Twenty-five shells at a clip."

"It shoots horizontally?"

"Dive bombers can come at you almost at ground level," he said. "This baby's ready for them at any altitude."

"How do you fire it?"

"The button is here," Cummins said, pointing to the handle of the weapon. "Go ahead, grab the handle and push the button in." He saw my hesitancy. "Hey, don't worry. Nothing happens until Johnson here feeds her the ammo."

Tentatively I wrapped my hand around the handle and placed a finger on the button.

KA-BOOOM!

I must have jumped three feet in the air, and when I came down both men were laughing uncontrollably. It took me a moment to realize why.

Darkness had fallen and as I looked skyward I could see that the evening's fireworks display had just begun.

68

Monday, July 5

I spent the morning writing articles for Wednesday's special *Morning News* section covering the history of the Soo Locks. Concentration was a real problem, though. My thoughts kept flashing to what I might find during my trip to Negaunee tomorrow.

The Canadian and American forces had just about given up their search for a German base in northern Canada. If the Krauts were going to launch an air attack from the north, there had to be evidence of some kind of airfield. But the military had combed the area as far north as Hudson Bay and east to the Atlantic without finding so much as a child's glider.

Mid-day we received rumor of a town meeting called for that evening in the banquet room above Blades Larue's restaurant. According to the local businessmen who had called the meeting, the purpose of the gathering was to make sure the town was prepared for the onslaught of people expected for the lock dedication just eleven days away. But G.P. guessed the real reason for the meeting ran deeper.

"The merchants are scared to death that people will stay away in droves if they get a whiff that there might be an attack on the locks," he said. "They've been threatening to organize a boycott of the News if we run a story that even hints that there might be some sort of danger at the dedication.

"Roland Swenson's been calling me all day with threats that Fred Westendorf, Tom Barbas or some other shopkeeper is going to cancel their advertising in the News if I don't back down. Personally, I think he's more worried than they are."

"What are we going to do?" I asked. As if I didn't know.
"Why, we're going to the meeting," G.P. announced.
We were going to stick our heads in the lion's mouth.

69

The sleek black Studebaker coupe slid past the shops on Ashman Street. The driver, James "Jimmy Shoes" Pecora, kept his focus on the woman on the sidewalk up ahead.

Jimmy Shoes thought she was classy, the way she walked. Real confident, like she knew exactly where she was going. Sharp dresser, too. Jimmy liked that. He earned his nickname from the expensive clothes he wore. You couldn't find clothes like that in a hick town like this. He had stopped at a few shops earlier, just to look around. You could buy a good pair of shoes in those shops for less than five bucks. Jimmy's cost five times that.

Yeah, the woman up ahead had to be her. He'd followed her from the time she left the *News* office. Joe Zerilli's boys had suspected she'd be in Sault Ste. Marie working for her uncle at the *Soo Morning News*. She fit the description they'd given him: five foot six, light brown hair, everything arranged precisely the way you'd want it.

She stopped now, and turned around. She looked at the Studebaker, then past it, down the street. A moment later she turned back and continued walking. Did she suspect he was tailing her? Probably not; but just to be sure he gunned the engine and drove past her, taking a right at the next corner onto Portage Street.

Jimmy Shoes felt certain the woman had to be Kate Brennan. He had found her, and for now that had to be enough. He had been driving all day for three days since leaving Cleveland. He was tired, and when you were tired you made mistakes.

He checked the address again on the paper in his pocket. One of Zerilli's capos, Danny Palazzolo, had pulled some strings to get him a place to stay. Danny told him that Sault Ste. Marie was packed with soldiers and civilians, but he had arranged for Jimmy to bunk in a rental cabin owned by his uncle.

Joe Zerilli, head of the "Partnership" as the Detroit mob called itself, had ordered a hit on the Brennan woman. Her series of *Times* articles had been honing in too close on the ration stamp counterfeiting that was netting the mob eleven million dollars every year. Rather than have one of his own soldiers carry out the mission, Zerilli had called his old friend, Alfred "Big Al" Polizzi, boss of the Cleveland mob. "I want the best button you have," he told Al. Polizzi said that would be Jimmy Shoes, and four days later Jimmy was here in Sault Ste. Marie.

Jimmy was twenty-nine. Most men his age were in the service, somewhere overseas. Had he been better educated, Jimmy would have termed it "ironic" that his criminal record had disqualified him, the best button in the Midwest, from killing Krauts overseas. There was nothing too serious on his rap sheet; maybe a couple armed robberies when he was a kid. He'd never come close to being convicted for the nearly two-dozen murders he'd pulled off since he became a made man.

Jimmy considered himself someone to be reckoned with, and he was. He had made his first mark at seventeen, killing a storeowner during one of his many armed robberies. The man pleaded for his life and Jimmy Shoes had said, "Okay, if you come to me on your knees and kiss my ring." As the man kissed his ring, he put a bullet through his head. They couldn't pin anything on him because there were no witnesses.

More killings followed, each more violent than the one that preceded it. They added up to twenty-three in all; soon the total would be twenty-four.

But now it was time for some rest.

70

Just before seven o'clock, G.P., Jack Crawford and I entered Blades' Tavern, walked past the bar and climbed the stairs. As we neared the top we could hear a rumble of voices. The meeting had attracted a crowd.

To our right, a well-stocked bar ran almost the 30-foot width of the far end of the room. There was an elevated platform against the wall to our left, with a polished wood dance floor directly in front of it. In between were tables, with chairs arranged around each one. The walls were knotty pine, like the tavern below, and the floor was brown tile.

A few of the windows were open, but the room still smelled of cigarette smoke and Spic 'n Span.

Scotty Banyon sat alone at one of the tables just off the dance floor and waved to us as we entered. We joined him, the men shaking hands and Scotty giving my hand a discrete squeeze as he motioned to the chair next to him. As we sat down a man who looked to be in his mid-forties stood and walked to the platform with a slight limp. He had dark hair and wore a navy blue suit with a light blue tie. I recognized him from photographs as Mayor Roland Swenson. The crowd quieted as he began to speak.

Swenson waded through a short preamble, thanking the crowd for coming, then threw the meeting open for comments from the floor.

Fred Westendorf, a tall, sandy-haired man in a light brown business suit that matched his hair stood at a table three feet from where we sat. He owned one of the two hardware stores in the Soo. "Tonight's meeting is supposed to be a planning session for the dedication ceremony," he began. "But I'd guess the reason most of us are here is the rumor that the Germans are planning an attack during the dedication ceremony."

It had taken all of 60 seconds for the real purpose of the meeting to surface. There was a murmur of agreement from many in the crowd.

Westendorf continued. "I for one don't buy it. I don't believe the Germans have planes capable of crossing the Atlantic, let alone flying here."

"It's been sixteen years since Lindberg made it across the Atlantic," called another man. "What makes you think the Krauts haven't developed planes that can fly that far?"

"Wait a minute," said a man at the table next to us. "They may not have to. I've heard talk that the Germans could be assembling small dive bombers piece by piece up in Canada."

"I've heard that both the Canadian Air Force and our Army Air Force have been searching without finding a thing," said Jim Danbert, owner of one of the Soo's many gift shops. "But, even if they did try an attack, the locks are well guarded. Why, our boys would blow them out of the sky."

G.P. cleared his throat as he stood, all eyes turning to him. "I think I know where this conversation is headed," he said. "I've heard some of you are against the Soo Morning News mentioning any word of a German threat."

There was another murmur from the crowd. G.P. held up a hand for silence.

"Some say we'll have two thousand people or more attending the dedication," he said. "Every one of them is at risk if the rumor turns out to be true."

"Now see here, G.P.," another shop owner, Rich Fabbiano, called out. "How do we know how true these rumors are? What if we scare people off, lose all the revenue they would have spent, and nothing happens?"

"I don't think we can take that chance." The speaker was Abe Lieberman, the local haberdasher. "I think we need to at least tell people what we know."

"Easy for you to say, Abe," said Fabbiano. "You don't risk much if the visitors leave. They're probably not buying suits and sport coats while they're here."

"I have as much at stake as you do, Rich," Lieberman said. "When visitors spend money here, it affects our town's whole economy. Folks like you have more money to spend on the clothes my store stocks."

"My drug store is already doing a swell business from people here for the dedication," said Jerry Dixon. "You publish some kind of b.s. about an attack, those people are going to leave." He looked around the room. "Sorry ladies," he said. Besides me, there were four other women present, owners of businesses around town.

"It's summer and ice cream sales are booming," said another man I didn't recognize. "Most of my buyers are from out of town."

"What do you think, Blades?" asked Westendorf. Blades' viewpoint would carry weight with quite a few of his fellow businessmen.

"Aw, hell," he said. "The more scared people are the more they drink. I'm in favor of letting them know there's at least a chance of an attack."

G.P. was still standing. "What if there is an attack and we've said nothing to warn people about it?" he asked. "The lives of men, women and even children are in our hands. If we fail to warn them about a danger, their deaths will be on our consciences."

The heated argument continued, with others jumping in on either side. G.P. seemed to have the final word when he announced that he alone determined the editorial content of the *Soo Morning News*. It seemed to quiet the crowd somewhat when he agreed to wait a few days before sounding an alarm. In the meantime, the source of an attack might be discovered and dealt with.

"Anyone else got something to say?" Swenson asked the crowd.

"Yeah," boomed Blades Larue. "The bar's open."

71

Blades' offer to buy the first round of drinks had a lot of takers. At least thirty of the fifty or so who had attended the meeting bellied up to the bar.

I was wary at first that the heat of the earlier discussions might turn into an ugly situation once people started drinking, but that wasn't the case. There were differences of opinion, alright, but most of them concerned whether a Squirrel Tail Streamer was more likely to catch rainbows than a Burlap Wiggler. Or which had the better brookie fishing between the Fox and Two Hearted Rivers.

Since I didn't know a fly rod from a bait bucket, most of the conversations were lost on me. I was glad when Scotty came over to the bar where I was standing nursing a Pfeiffer's Beer and smoking a Chesterfield.

"I see you're keeping your fishing expertise to yourself," he said with a smile. "Not everyone is that modest." He motioned to a crowd down the bar where two women had joined the men in an animated conversation that obviously had something to do with fishing. One of the women was making exaggerated motions of reeling in what had to be a gigantic trout.

"You might be surprised," I said. "In fact, I've got a whale of a fishing story for you." I told Scotty about the trip to Negaunee I planned to make over the next few days. I told him what I had found out concerning Shirley and I included what little I knew about the mystery of the Stop Inn and its equally mysterious proprietor.

"Be careful, Kate," he said when I'd finished. "There's something that doesn't sound right about all this."

I started to agree, but my thoughts were interrupted when I heard Abe Lieberman, standing in the crowd beside us, mention a stranger he had seen hanging around the downtown area near Ashmun Street. I had noticed the same stranger, and maybe it was paranoia, but he seemed to be watching me. The guy had been dressed in an expensive suit and tie, definitely not your average Sault Ste. Marie native. In fact, he stood out like a clown at a funeral.

"I've seen him, too," said Westendorf. "A fellow like him is hard to miss in this town. Drives a black Studebaker. Sharp dresser, too. He sure didn't buy those clothes here." He glanced sheepishly at Lieberman. "Sorry, Abe."

Westendorf turned to my uncle. "Do you know anything about him, G.P.? I hear he's been asking questions about the Soo Morning News."

"Don't know a thing," said G.P. "In fact I don't recall seeing anyone like that."

"I have," I said, and suddenly it seemed all eyes had turned my way. I felt the need to elaborate. "When I was downstate I ran into some trouble with the mob. I can spot their type, and that guy fits the mold."

"I heard he's staying in one of Jack Palazzolo's cabins," Rich Fabbiano said. "Been up here a day or so."

I was glad when the conversation shifted to other topics and felt foolish for even mentioning my run-in with the mob. I downplayed the subject when Crawford brought it up later. But I couldn't help mentioning it as Scotty and I were leaving the bar. He had walked me to my car, and we were talking and sharing a goodnight kiss or two to make up for my being away for the next couple of days.

"I think you're making too much of the guy," Scotty said. "I'll bet he's gone in a day or two and we forget all about him."

"I hope you're right," I said.

But I feared he was wrong.

72

Tuesday, July 6

Next morning Mick and I were on our way to Negaunee in my thirty-seven Ford. I confess I exceeded the 35 mph speed limit whenever I could. Sorry Mr. President.

I've heard plenty of people from other places brag about their state's beauty, but to me there's nothing quite like Michigan; especially the Upper Peninsula. It possesses an unspoiled splendor you won't find anywhere else. Gently rolling hills, Tahquamenon Falls, the Pictured Rocks where you look down on a dazzling blue Lake Superior from cliffs a hundred feet high.

I had chosen a more direct route along Highway 28, miles south of the lake, and found myself in those gently rolling hills surrounded by green - oaks, maples, birch and lots of northern pine. My car windows were down and I could smell the sweetness of the forest as I drove. Mick had his head out the back window and I could just imagine the cacophony of aromas his sensitive nose was taking in.

We stopped for gas at a Cities Service station in McMillan and I fed Mick and let him out for some exercise. Thankfully, Jack Crawford had provided me with a few gasoline stamps from the newspaper's supply. A small restaurant sat next door to the service station and I had a bite to eat. We were on our way again a half hour later.

We arrived in Negaunee around suppertime and I decided to drop into the Stop Inn restaurant to eat. But when I found the address that had been given on Shirley's resume, it wasn't a restaurant at all; it was a brown two-story home. I knocked and received the surprise of my life when a woman appeared at the door.

It was the woman I had seen at Shirley's funeral.

73

The woman stood about five foot three and wore her hair tucked in a bun on the back of her head. I had to talk to her through a screen door.

"Mrs. Wilson?"

"I'm sorry, I can't help you," she said just before she slammed the front door in my face.

I knocked again, with no result. I walked around the corner of the house, hoping to catch someone's attention through one of the windows. Mrs. Wilson had anticipated me, though, and all the shades were drawn. Reaching the backyard, I climbed the short steps to the back door and knocked there with the same negative result.

I felt famished, and I knew Mick had to be just as hungry. I decided to regroup: we'd find a place to stay for the night, have a bite to eat and then I'd come back here with hopes of finding out why Mrs. Wilson insisted on being so inhospitable.

I retraced the route back toward town and found a collection of tourist cabins on a small lake just outside of town. Luckily they welcomed pets. I took Mick for a walk in the tall weeds beside the cabin we'd rented and then left him inside with water and a large ceramic bowl filled with dry dog food.

I ordered fish and chips in a small restaurant on Iron Street across from the Vista Theater and I chewed over my current situation while I ate. Obviously there was no Stop Inn; at least not in Negaunee. But just as big a mystery was Mrs. Wilson's reaction. Why had she acted so rudely?

After driving the better part of a day to get to Negaunee, I wasn't going to meekly turn tail and retreat back to the Soo. There was still enough daylight left to allow another try at Mrs. Wilson after supper.

74

When I got to the Wilson's home again, I parked my car in the drive, walked to the door and knocked.

No reply. I knocked again, and then decided to try the back door. As I rounded the house I noticed the door of the garage standing behind the house was open and the building was empty.

I mounted the few steps to the back door and knocked. Again I was greeted by silence.

I was getting mad. In desperation, I tried the door handle and found it unlocked. The door swung open slightly, and I called inside.

"Mrs. Wilson?"

No answer. I'm not a thief, but after driving all the way from the Soo, I was not about to go home without solving the mystery of the non-existent Stop Inn and its rude proprietor. I opened the door all the way and stepped through into a small kitchen. A refrigerator and gas stove stood on my right, a sink to my left. The aroma of fresh-baked pastry filled the room. I walked to the oven and opened it, feeling the handle warm. Sure enough, inside was a pie; still warm. The Wilson's hadn't been gone long.

The shades were drawn on the window above the sink and the house was dim, but not dark. The summer sun still bore in through the shaded windows.

I walked past the kitchen into a small dining area, again calling for anyone who might be home. I passed a closed door on my right and walked to an open doorway just ahead. Peering inside the room, I found a double bed and dresser set that obviously belonged to Mr. and Mrs. Wilson.

Feeling like Goldilocks invading the home of the three bears, I turned back and walked to the door I had just passed. I tried the handle and found it open. It appeared to be the bedroom of a teen-aged girl. There were three teddy bears on the carefully made bed and the wallpaper was covered with flowery prints. On top of the plain wood dresser was a photograph. The three smiling faces were Shirley and the two people I had seen at her funeral. The woman was the Mrs. Wilson who had slammed the door in my face.

When I saw them at the Soo, I thought they had been Shirley's aunt and uncle. But Shirley had spoken about her mother's sister and her husband often and I was sure their name was Bergman, not Wilson.

I picked up the photograph and looked at my old friend; then I gazed around the room. The papers were neatly placed on the small desk next to the bed, and there were a few knickknacks on the dresser and windowsill. A University of Michigan pennant adorned the wall over the bed. Shirley had clearly lived here in this room at one time and it looked as if she were expected to return any minute.

I couldn't help noticing what looked like a thick scrapbook setting on the desk. I picked it up and began thumbing through. Page after page of the book was filled with yellowed clippings of newspaper articles featuring a U.S. Congressman Neil Roberts of Ann Arbor.

Some of the stories had photos of the congressman and his constituents. There were quite a few of him cutting ribbons at the opening of local businesses or shaking hands with a mayor or some other politician. I turned another page and there was a clipping with a photo of the congressman with Shirley. The caption identified Shirley as the congressman's "personal assistant."

That explained Shirley's life immediately after college. But the dates on the clippings that started in September of 1932, ended abruptly in 1937. What happened after that remained a mystery. There was nothing here that hinted at what she became involved in afterwards.

And it raised some nagging questions: why did Shirley make up a story about flunking out of school? Why didn't she mention Congressman Neil Roberts? Why did she falsify her resume to show she had been employed at a non-existent restaurant?

And what had brought her back to the Soo as a waitress?

Those thoughts were on my mind when the world suddenly went dark.

75

In what I now realize was a dream, Shirley was alive and we were both back in high school English class. The teacher, who looked exactly like Mrs. Wilson, stood in front of the class with the same stern look she had worn when she answered her front door.

Mrs. Wilson had caught Shirley and me whispering to each other during her lecture and she grabbed Shirley gruffly by the arm and pulled her toward the door. Shirley tried desperately to hold onto her desk, but her hands slipped and the teacher dragged her off into the hall.

As the classroom door slammed shut, someone was coughing violently nearby; then I heard voices I didn't recognize. Real voices.

"Those cigarettes are gonna kill you."

"I know."

"You ought to quit."

"I've tried. It's tough."

My nose was taking in the distinct aroma of alcohol that reminded me of a dentist's office. I opened my eyes and saw two faces staring down at me. As the scene came into focus, I realized the face just above me belonged to a man in his fifties who wore a white doctor's smock. He had a wreath of white hair around an otherwise shiny head and wore a white mustache. Standing beside him was another man who appeared to be in his mid-twenties. He wore a brown shirt with a bronze badge pinned to it and had the dark hair and complexion of an American Indian.

I tried to sit up but my body weighed a ton. I flopped backwards onto the bed. I tried to talk but words came as gibberish.

"Just relax, Miss Brennan. I'm Doctor Reynolds. This is Deputy Hightower. You're in the county hospital."

I rubbed my forehead with my left hand. "How did I get here?"

"Mr. and Mrs. Bergman phoned our office," said the deputy. "They found you passed out in their home."

"Mr. and Mrs. Bergman?" So that *was* the home of Shirley's uncle and aunt.

"We picked you up by ambulance and brought you here," the deputy said.

I tried to remember what had happened. The last thing I could picture was a scrapbook with newspaper clippings of the congressman and Shirley. Then. . .? Nothing.

"What happened to me?"

"You were unconscious," said the doctor. "Most likely you were drugged. There was a slight odor of chloroform in the room."

"Who would have done that?"

The deputy shook his head. "We were hoping you could tell us. There was no one else in the house when the Bergmans got home."

My head was beginning to clear and I tried to sit up again.

"Easy," said the doctor. He put his hand around my back and helped me sit upright.

As I shook the cobwebs out of my brain, reality slowly came back into focus. I thought of Mick cooped up back at the cabin by the lake. "I've got to get out of here."

"You'll have to stay, ma'am. You're under arrest."

"Arrest? For what?"

"Breaking into the Bergman's home."

"I didn't break in. The door was unlocked."

"Just the same," he said, "you entered without permission."

"But I was a close friend of their niece's." Despite the doubt on the faces of both men, I went on. "Shirley Benoit, the Bergman's niece and my best friend, was murdered a week ago in Sault Ste. Marie. I was looking for some sort of clue that might tell who did it."

The deputy still looked doubtful. "You think her uncle or aunt killed her?"

"Of course not. I didn't even realize the house belonged to the Bergmans. I was just looking into her background to see if there was a clue to someone who might want her dead. For some reason or another.

"Will you please call them for me? Tell them who I am?"

"I'll try." The deputy started to leave.

"Wait. Before you go, you don't happen to have a cigarette I could borrow, do you?"

The deputy shook his head. "Sorry. I don't smoke."

"Here," said the doctor, reaching into his breast pocket, "take one of mine."

The deputy reappeared a few moments later. "The Bergmans say they never heard of you. They're going to press charges."

"If I could just talk to them. . ."

"I'm afraid they don't want to talk to you," said the deputy. "They've said as much. You do, however, have the right to make a phone call."

I was considering whether to call my uncle or Scotty when a thought struck me.

"Deputy, will you call the Bergmans for me again?"

"I'm afraid it won't do any good, ma'am. They seemed very adamant."

"I think it will, if you mention a certain word to them."

"What word?"

"Snuggles."

76

"How do you know about Snuggles?"

Mrs. Wilson, now Mrs. Bergman, stood beside my bed. At her left was Mr. Bergman; tall, rather slim and wearing rimless glasses. Mrs. Bergman was shorter and wore her hair back in a bun. Seeing them standing side by side was like viewing a living copy of Grant Wood's *American Gothic*.

"Mrs. Bergman, this is all a terrible mistake. Shirley and I were best friends. We graduated together from Soo High."

"Shirley never mentioned you, Kathryn. You couldn't have been best friends."

"Kathryn? My name is Kate. Kate Brennan."

"You're Kate Brennan?" Mrs. Bergman appeared shocked.

"Yes, of course."

"We didn't dream . . . your drivers' license said Kathryn Brennan, not Kate," said Mr. Bergman. "And your home address is Detroit, not the Soo."

"It's Detroit now," I said. "But I lived with my uncle in Sault Ste. Marie during my senior year in high school. And my friends knew me as Kate . . . not Kathryn or Kathy."

"Shirley did mention Kate Brennan; many times. You and Shirley must have been very close for her to tell you . . . you know, Snuggles."

"We were very close."

Mrs. Bergman's stern look reappeared. "What were you doing in our home?"

"I'm sorry. Shirley's resume had listed the Stop Inn at your address as her last place of employment. When I saw it was a private home and not a restaurant I got suspicious. I was trying to find some clues that might lead to the person who killed her."

Mrs. Bergman turned to the deputy. "If we don't press charges, can Miss Brennan leave now?"

The deputy shook his head. "I don't know, Mrs. Berman. Sheriff Sandstrum would have to approve that and he's over in Marquette for the next two days."

"Deputy Hightower, I've known you since you were a boy," Mrs. Bergman said. "And I also know Sheriff Sandstrum's jail has just one cell. Isn't that right?"

The deputy began to blush. "Well . . . yes."

"How many prisoners are you holding?"

"Three. But . . ."

"And I'm sure they're all male. Where are you going to house Miss Brennan? The doctor isn't going to keep her here if she's healthy enough to leave."

The deputy was backed into a corner. His arms were crossed in front of him, his face wore a frown.

"Let me see if I can reach the Sheriff."

"You do that, deputy," said Mrs. Bergman. "Meantime, Miss Brennan will be in our custody. She's going home with us."

77

My car was still where I had left it when we pulled into the gravel driveway of the Bergman's house. We had picked up Mick on the way, and he and I took up most of the backseat of the Bergman's '36 Chevy.

The Bergmans didn't object when Mick followed us into their house, in fact they seemed to enjoy having a dog around. The four of us sat in the small, but comfortable living room. There was a vase of flowers on the coffee table along with issues of *Life* and *National Geographic*.

"May I ask why Shirley listed this address as her former place of employment?" I said. "It's obviously not a restaurant."

The Bermans looked at each other before Mr. Bergman spoke. "You and Shirley knew each other in high school," he said. "What do you know about Shirley's life afterwards?"

"Not much," I said.

Mr. Bergman paused again, carefully choosing his words.

"When Shirley graduated from the University of Michigan, she joined the staff of Neil Roberts, the U.S. Representative from the Ann Arbor district."

"She followed Roberts to Washington. What happened between them I don't know. Could have been a romantic relationship that didn't work out. Anyway, Shirley left him and joined the Federal Bureau of Investigation in thirty-nine."

"The FBI?" I was shocked.

"Yes. The fact that she joined the Bureau was strictly hush-hush," Mr. Bergman continued. "But as her closest living relatives, we of course knew. We were questioned during their background check."

"At first, she was assigned to Atlanta, Georgia," said Mrs. Bergman.

"But the Bureau apparently feared some sort of attack on the locks, and she come up here to Sault Ste. Marie.

"It seemed important to Shirley to keep her identity with the FBI a secret," Mrs. Bergman continued. "But she'd call us from time to time, and visited for a few days last April. She never went into any great detail, but she seemed grateful to have someone to talk to. Someone who knew her situation."

"We're telling you this now only because you were a friend of Shirley's and because . . ." Mr. Bergman paused, gathering himself. "Because it doesn't seem to matter now that she's gone."

"Shirley's friends would be proud to know she was serving her country when she died," I said.

"Shirley felt taking a job as a waitress in a popular restaurant would give her a listening post," Mrs. Berman said. "People often converse during a meal with little thought to who's listening; especially their waitress."

"She needed a history of previous employment, so we made up the Stop Inn," Mr. Bergman said. He smiled. "The name was my idea. Shirley liked it."

"The name 'Mrs. Wilson' was a code of sorts," said Mrs. Bergman. "If someone called asking for Mrs. Wilson we'd know we were supposed to act like the proprietors of the Stop Inn. When you called, we were caught off guard; we got suspicious. Why would anyone be asking about the Stop Inn now?" She paused, wiping her eyes with a handkerchief. "I mean now that Shirley's gone."

"I don't understand what's taking them so long to find the killer," Mr. Berman said. "The newspapers say the soldier the sheriff arrested turned out to be innocent."

"That's right," I said. "They don't seem to have any other leads."

"Why, what about Shirley's journal?" Mrs. Bergman asked. "That ought to give them some clues."

"Journal?" Shirley had never mentioned one to me.

"Shirley told us she kept details of her investigation in some sort of journal," Mrs. Bergman said. "If the person who killed her had anything to do with that investigation, I'm sure her journal would provide some answers."

My suspicions that an intruder had searched Shirley's house for something other than money came roaring back.

"The authorities don't have Shirley's journal," I said. "I don't think they even know it exists. Who else besides you two knew about it, Mrs. Bergman?"

"As far as I know, we're the only ones. Shirley kept things like that to herself. She mentioned the journal when she was here in April."

"I'll look for it when I get back to the Soo," I said. "I'll go over the house inch by inch." I didn't mention the fact that someone else had probably already done that.

It was suppertime and there was no point in keeping the Bergmans from their meal. It was time to leave.

"Thank you so much for trusting me," I said, standing up. "You've been a great help."

"Shirley spoke about you so fondly that I feel we know you," said Mrs. Bergman. "And you remind me very much of her. I was fixing a beef roast when the deputy called and I can have it back in the oven in a jiffy. Won't you stay for dinner?"

I've never been one to turn down a home-cooked meal.

78

The Bergmans invited me to stay the night, but I decided that with Mick and all, it would be better to go back to the cabin I'd rented.

As I lay in bed later that night, a chilling thought went through my head. I knew from experience that Joe Zerilli and his mob cohorts wanted me out of the picture. That's what got me to the Soo in the first place.

Now there seemed to be a suspicious stranger in town. How long had he been there?

Shirley and I had looked enough alike to be mistaken for each other from time to time. Could Shirley have been murdered by mistake? Was the stranger really after me?

The idea sent a shiver through my spine.

But then my thoughts returned to Shirley's work with the FBI. It seemed much more logical that she had been murdered in the line of duty. If the Bergmans were correct, the answers lay in a journal she had been keeping. I vowed to find it when I got back to the Soo.

If Shirley's murderer hadn't already beaten me to it.

79

Wednesday evening, Sault Ste. Marie

Where was Kate Brennan?

The clock on the bed stand marked the time at ten-thirty p.m. and Jimmy Shoes Pecora paced the floor of the rented cabin. He'd grown tired of hanging around this hick town; it was time to get the job done and get the hell out of Sault Ste. Marie.

A city boy all his life, Pecora found the wilderness of northern Michigan unsettling. This was country that stretched for miles without buildings or even people. Country inhabited by huge moose, bear and coyote. A country bordering on a body of water that was more ocean than lake. He had read that depths in Lake Superior plunged almost fifteen hundred feet in places and its violent November storms were known to devour giant freighters and the men who sailed them.

There was something else. Maybe just nerves, but he had the feeling over the past day or so that someone was following him. He was tailing the Brennan woman, and someone was tailing him.

Then Kate Brennan disappeared. Fearing she had gotten wise to him, he phoned the *News*, posing as a reader who wanted her to do a story on a giant bass he had caught in the St. Marys River.

"Sorry, Kate's not in the office today," said the woman who answered the phone. "She won't be back here until late tomorrow afternoon. But we can send one of our other reporters to interview you." Jimmy Shoes hung up. Knowing the Brennan woman would be back tomorrow made him feel better. He'd be heading back to Cleveland soon.

He glanced around the small cabin. He felt restless, not at all ready to sleep. He noticed a web in the corner of the cabin and walked over to it. At first it appeared to be just a cobweb, but then he saw the spider, almost invisible against the dark wood of the wall.

In the web was an insect, probably a fly, wrapped in silk and ready to serve as the arachnid's breakfast tomorrow morning.

Percora heard buzzing near the top of the window just to his right. A fly. He reached up and, when the insect landed for a brief moment, took a swipe at it. He missed, but caught it when it landed on the window a second time.

He reached into his fist with the thumb and index finger of his other hand and watched the fly as it moved its legs in panic, trying desperately to escape. He reached down and tossed the insect into the spider's web.

The spider raced out to greet it, holding the fly to its mouth, biting and then wrapping it in a sheet of silk.

Lunch.

Pecora glanced around the cabin looking for another victim.

A knock at the door interrupted his thoughts.

80

The knock startled him. Who could know he was here besides Palazzolo's uncle, and what the hell would anyone want at ten-thirty at night?

Pecora strode to the door and opened it a crack, peering out into the darkness, seeing no one. Must have been his imagination; he closed the door.

Looking about the cabin again, he spotted a tiny white moth fluttering against the window over the sink. Pecora grabbed it with a single swipe and walked back to the web. He threw the moth into the web and enjoyed watching as it struggled helplessly against the silk strands. The spider raced over and soon the thrashing ended.

Supper.

Another knock. This time he was sure. He flung the door open, ready to confront whoever stood there.

No one.

Who was stupid enough to play games with Jimmy Pecora? Whoever it was would pay dearly. He walked to the chair that held his coat and gun. He pulled the suit coat over his bare torso and took the .38 from the holster that hung on the chair.

Outside, he reached through the open window of the Studebaker's passenger side and retrieved a flashlight from the glove box. Playing the light around the front of the small brown log cabin, he saw no one. The next cabin stood thirty feet away and its lights were out. Behind the string of cabins lay a thick forest. He decided to look for the intruder there.

The night was cool and Jimmy Shoes tugged the coat tightly around him. He jumped involuntarily as the hoot of an owl broke the silence. He continued on, reaching the rear of the cabin. The forest loomed twenty feet beyond.

As he began walking in the direction of the forest, he heard a rustling behind him. Turning, he was startled to see that the dim light shining through the blackout curtain of his cabin's rear window framed the silhouette of a large man.

"Who are you?" he asked. Something about the man made him nervous and he was surprised to hear his voice cracking as he spoke. "What the hell do you want?"

As the stranger approached, Jimmy shined the flashlight on him and could clearly see the features of the man's face. For the first time in his life Jimmy Shoes was confronted by someone who didn't seem afraid of him. Or of the pistol he held.

Jimmy Shoes' last thought on earth was how odd that was. And how odd it was that the man actually smiled when he spoke.

"Mein name ist Claus Krueger."

81

Thursday, July 8
Three days before the dedication

Mick and I got an early start from Negaunee and arrived back at the Soo late that afternoon. I let Mick out in the backyard and began searching the house thoroughly for Shirley's journal; hoping whoever had broken into the house days ago hadn't beaten me to it.

I went through the first and second floors as I had before, this time much more carefully. I knocked on walls here and there as I had seen detectives do in the movies, listening for a hollow sound that might be the clue to a secret compartment.

Finding nothing, I went down into the basement. Shirley's basement was unfinished, the cinderblock walls painted white. I searched the perimeter, looking for tiny cracks in the cement between blocks. Perhaps one was a false door leading to a small storage space.

No luck.

The generous space under the washtub made it easy to see nothing had been hidden there. The workbench in the far corner yielded zip, zero, zed and a goose egg as I ran through its four drawers.

So much for the basement.

I searched the attic again with the same result. Shirley's bedroom was next to mine on the main floor and I left it for last. I went through her closet item by item finding nothing.

Her chest of drawers proved equally uneventful, just the usual assortment of blouses and underclothes.

Shirley's jewelry box contained a variety of earrings, bracelets and a couple of necklaces. As I sat on her bed going through the items, I picked up a necklace Shirley had worn constantly in high school. It was heart-shaped, and when I snapped it open my eyes started to tear. The necklace contained a picture of her father and mother who had been killed in that tragic automobile accident. When closed, it was as if they were kissing. I sat for a moment, my eyes watering, as I realized what that locket must have meant to Shirley, a teenager coping with life without parents.

I could identify with her, because I had been left in the care of my uncle. But when my emotions got the best of me, I could at least talk with my father on the telephone. Shirley couldn't. It must have been terribly lonely. I sat there on her bed for a while, my feelings washing over me.

Then it was time to get back to reality. I finished my search of the house and came up empty on every count. Either the intruder had found the journal days ago, or Shirley had hidden it somewhere else.

I had missed Scotty while I was gone and thought about looking him up. But first I'd check in with G.P. and Crawford at the office.

82

"He was a mob hit man and someone treated him like a schoolboy," G.P. was saying. He leaned back in his chair, his head nearly touching the American flag in the stand behind him.

"The man's neck was broken very cleanly," G.P. continued. "Whoever did it was incredibly strong. And fast. There was a loaded .38 caliber pistol lying next to him. Whoever did him in never gave him a chance to use it."

"Where did the murder take place?" I asked.

"Outside one of Palazzolo's rental cabins," G.P. said. "Crawford found the body."

"Did I hear someone mention my name?"

I turned to see Jack Crawford standing in the doorway, shirtsleeves rolled up, tie loosened.

"I was just telling Kate about our friend who the authorities say is Jimmy Shoes Pecora."

"He bumped into someone who wasn't very friendly," Crawford said. "Who was the guy, anyway?"

"I'm sure it was the fellow everyone talked about the other night at Blades Larue's place. Sheriff says he was the Cleveland mob's best hit man. 'Button men,' they call them," G.P. said.

"Cleveland, huh? Any idea what he was doing up here?" Crawford asked.

Knowing my background with the mob, both men turned to me. "He might have been looking for me," I said. "Detroit and Cleveland mobs have been known to work closely together. Maybe they figured I'd recognize one of their Detroit thugs and they recruited one from Cleveland."

"So you think he was here to deal with you?" G.P. asked.

I shrugged. "They tried it back in Detroit. It's not far-fetched to think they'd track me up here."

I turned to Crawford with a reporter's question. "How'd you happen to find Pecora's body?"

"Couldn't sleep," he said. "Went for a walk. Found the body near one of the rental cabins just outside of town."

"That's a long walk from where you're staying at G.P.'s house," I said.

"I was in the mood for a long walk. As I said, I couldn't sleep."

"Jack and I stayed up late talking," said G.P. "Jack retired for the evening, but got up again about a half hour later. I saw him go out for a walk."

"What time was that?" I asked.

G.P. turned to Crawford. "What do you think, Jack? Eleven thirty?"

"Sounds right."

It sounded strange to me. My uncle was an early riser and in all the years I'd known him he never stayed up later than nine or ten o'clock.

83

Friday, July 9
Two days before the dedication

Scotty's big blowout aboard the Caiman was scheduled for Friday evening, and I looked forward to it with anticipation. With a crowd of notables in town for the dedication of the MacArthur Lock, the guest list promised to overflow with dignitaries. Not to mention the fact that I planned to spend as much time as possible with the host. That is, if he still wanted me to. Scotty had begged off seeing me when I called last night, saying he was busy with last minute preparations. I hoped that story was true and he wasn't just making up something to avoid me.

My car windows were down as I drove into the Riverbend Marina's gravel parking lot. I was wearing a stylish black dress I thought fit the occasion, topped off with a pearl necklace I inherited from my Aunt Betty. A small musical group was playing *Boogie Woogie Bugle Boy* on the deck above the Caiman's fantail and I could see a few people in a dancing frenzy in front of the band.

Scotty couldn't have picked a more perfect evening. The sun shone brightly in the western sky and I could smell the crispness of the gentle breeze blowing in from the St. Marys River. Almost a mile across the river lay the endless tree line of Sugar Island.

I heard talking and laughter coming from inside the Caiman as I strolled up the gangplank, once more dazzled by the immensity of Scotty's yacht.

The Caiman's salon was packed with people talking in small clusters, dressed to the nines and holding their Tom Collins, high balls and Scotch and waters. There was a smattering of uniforms, mostly higher ranking officers from Fort Brady. Chef Joseph and an assistant fussed over a buffet table positioned against the far wall.

Some of the guests I knew, some I didn't. Blades Larue stood in a group that included Len Townes, Bill Milton and their wives. Standing in a small group next to them were two men I recognized from photographs as the U.S. Congressman from the district and our State Senator. A third member looked a lot like our former U.S. Senator.

I recognized a couple of newspaper reporters from downstate holding up the bar and walked over to say hello. A week ago I would have worried about blowing my cover, but if my suspicions about Pecora were correct, the mob already knew too well where to find me.

Bill Ronson of the *Detroit News* was the first to wave a greeting. "Why, Kate Brennan! You left us all wondering where the hell you were."

"Say," said Curt Neumann, "Harry Houdini would have loved your vanishing act." Neumann was a veteran reporter who had been with the *Cleveland Plain Dealer* before deciding to join the *Associated Press* wire service and moving to the Arsenal of Democracy. Although he had me by at least twenty years in the age department, his ready sense of humor had made us fast friends.

"It was getting a little too warm around Detroit," I said. "I decided to come up here to cool off." I chose not to mention that someone from the mob had created a bit of unwelcome heat up here, too.

"Who's here from the Times?" I asked.

"Stan Dreslinski," said Bill Ronson. "We're staying together in a hotel across the river in Canada. Your town is filled."

"Where is he?"

Bill laughed. "We came in separate vehicles. He had a little trouble crossing the border. He was just ahead of us driving off the car ferry. The customs officials asked him if he had anything to declare."

"Yeah?"

"He told them, and I quote, 'Only my love for Canada and all things Canadian.' They're probably still searching his car."

"That sounds like Stan," I laughed. "But Wells is going to raise the roof if he doesn't file a story."

"He'll be along," said Curt Neumann. "I think he learned a hard lesson. You don't mess with the Border Patrol during a world war."

Curt then introduced me to the others in the group, treating them to a brief description of my series of articles and subsequent troubles with the Detroit mob.

"Detroit's not the only city with that kind of crime problem," Curt said. "I covered the Cleveland mob for the Plain Dealer. 'Big Al' Polizzi runs the show, there."

We traded Zerilli and Polizzi stories for a while, before I excused myself and walked aft through the cabin door to the fantail. I found Scotty there chatting with some of the townspeople. He looked smashing in a gold blazer that matched the color of his hair, and a tie that accented his blue eyes perfectly. A waiter passed by carrying a tray of champagne and I reached for one of the glasses. Scotty excused himself from the group and walked over to me.

"I was hoping you'd make it," he said. I felt a tingle as he leaned over and kissed me on the cheek. The evening was starting off just as I had hoped. I tried to act nonchalant.

"Just try and keep me away," I said breezily. "By the looks of your guest list, I should feel honored to be here."

"We expected Governor Kelly," Scotty said. "But he was kept in Lansing with some last minute business. He'll be aboard Sunday."

"Where are all these people staying? I heard the hotels around here are all booked up."

"They are," said Scotty. "But I reserved the whole top floor of the Ojibway two months ago. By the way, how was Negaunee?"

"I want to talk with you about it later."

The fantail seemed as crowded as the salon. Scotty pointed to a group near the back rail that included G.P. and several other men. "Your uncle looks like he could use some help and I've got to check on the buffet," he said. "I'll join you in a minute."

I walked back to the group where an animated discussion was taking place. Mayor Roland Swenson was waving a finger at my uncle.

"I'm telling you, G.P., stories of an attack on the locks are going to hurt business in this town. People sense danger and they won't come anywhere near Sault Ste. Marie."

"People have a right to know what's going on," G.P. said. "Who knows? Blades might be right; you might even draw a bigger crowd. People are funny that way."

"Business is booming," said another of the men. "People are already coming into town for Sunday's dedication. Why take a chance of ruining that?"

"What if the threat is real?" G.P. said. "What if just one plane gets past the artillery? Why, there will be thousands there to watch the ceremony. Every life will be at risk."

"I seriously doubt a plane could get past all those heavy guns," said the mayor. "In fact, I'd like to see the Krauts try."

Scotty joined the group just in time. "Chef Joseph says the buffet's ready, gentlemen. Don't keep the prime rib waiting."

The conversation halted as the participants headed toward the salon.

84

The crowd had thinned by ten o'clock. Some had bid their goodnights; others had gone to dance on the upper deck. I could hear the band topside playing *I'll be Seeing You.* Scotty and I stood among a small group lingering on the fantail that included G.P., Jack Crawford and a dozen or so others.

The sun had disappeared and ambient light shone from a string of small, colorful bulbs strung along the roof of the fantail, turning faces shades of reds, blues and greens.

The earlier argument of whether the newspaper should warn of a possible attack on the locks had been revived shortly after the meal. G.P. ended it quickly, telling the mayor he alone determined what stories the *Soo Morning News* ran. I didn't know it then, but he had already written an editorial for tomorrow's edition discussing the subject.

I had wanted to talk with Jack Crawford about finding Jimmy Pecora's body; I still had suspicions he wasn't being entirely truthful. Something about his story just didn't add up. But he seemed to be avoiding me. I noticed Curt Neumann chatting with him briefly and thought of walking over to them, but Crawford quickly excused himself and went to the bar for a refill.

A bit later, Curt sauntered up to me, by now slightly inebriated. "Kate, that guy, Jack Crawford. He's your boss, isn't he?"

"Yes. Why do you ask?"

"How well do you know him?"

"Not well at all. I've only been here in the Soo a matter of weeks."

"He claims he worked for the Cleveland News Courier."

"Yes. Until last December, I believe."

"Kate, I have friends back in Cleveland who work for the News

Courier."

"Yes?"

"I asked Crawford if he knew them."

"Didn't he?"

"Yes, but his answers seemed a bit vague. So I decided to test him. I made up a name and asked Crawford if he knew the man."

"And he said he did?"

"Yes. But I think he must have suspected I was on to him. He excused himself and went to the bar. Never came back.

"Kate, Jack Crawford never worked for the Courier. I'd bet my last dollar on that."

85

Something smelled fishy and it wasn't the wind blowing in off the St. Marys River.

Regardless of the fact that Curt Neumann had been over served at the bar, his conviction that Jack Crawford hadn't worked for the *News Courier* alarmed me.

I decided to check it out. I saw G.P. near the door of the fantail saying good-bye to two of the congressmen and walked over.

"Big weekend coming up," I heard him say. "Got to get my beauty sleep."

I caught his eye and motioned that I wanted to talk a moment before he left. He finished with the politicians and came over to me.

"What is it, Kate?"

"It's Jack Crawford," I said. "He had a conversation a while ago with a reporter I know who worked for the Cleveland Plain Dealer at one time. He's convinced Crawford never worked for the News Courier."

G.P.'s face tightened. "Kate, Jack Crawford's references were, and are, impeccable. I checked them thoroughly myself."

My face must have registered doubt, because my uncle spoke again. "Kate, the Soo Morning News has been my entire life since your Aunt Susan died. Do you think I'd hire anyone who wouldn't be good for the paper?"

I had to admit he was right.

Later, Scotty and I were dancing on the upper deck to the band's final number when I mentioned my thoughts about Crawford.

"I think you're letting your imagination get the best of you," Scotty said. "Crawford seems like a good egg.

"By the way, how was your expedition to Negaunee?"

I had wanted to tell Scotty about the trip earlier and hadn't gotten the chance. He and I had grown close over the past week and I felt comfortable confiding in him.

"Shirley was working for the FBI," I said.

Scotty pulled back and looked me in the eye. "You're joking," he said.

"I found Shirley's aunt and uncle in Negaunee. They told me all about it."

And I proceeded to tell Scotty everything I had learned from the Bergmans.

"I'm truly shocked," Scotty said when I'd finished. "As serious as she seemed to be about our relationship, Shirley never breathed a word to me about working for the FBI. What about that diary the Bergmans mentioned? Do you have it?"

"No," I said, "and it worries me. The dedication ceremony is just two days away. If there's going to be an attack, the records Shirley kept might help us avoid it."

"You've searched Shirley's house, of course."

"Of course. And I'm not the only one."

"What do you mean?" Scotty asked.

I told him that someone had searched Shirley's home shortly after her death, and that whoever it was, wasn't after money.

"Let me know if you find that diary."

"I will."

"After all, if there *is* an attack the Caiman is going to be in harm's way."

"If there's an attack, we'll all be in harm's way, Scotty."

A bit later Scotty walked me to my car, one of the few remaining in the parking lot. We kissed, very passionately I thought. When we came up for air he asked me to stay with him that night aboard the Caiman.

"I'll be tied up from tomorrow morning until after the dedication," he said. "I won't see you until then."

"I would love to stay, Scotty," I said, and I really meant it. "But tomorrow's a full day for me too. I promised to meet Andy Checkle early in the morning. We're working on a special edition for the dedication Sunday.

"But hold that thought. We'll do it when all the hoopla of this weekend is over."

Driving home, I felt certain I had made the right decision - about this evening, and about letting Scotty into my life. Memories of Ronny would always be an inseparable part of me. They would never die.

But I had finally come to grips with the fact that Ronny had.

86

Saturday, July 10
One day before the Dedication

Dedication Attendees Deserve a Warning

An editorial by G.P. Brennan
Publisher, Soo Morning News

Hundreds of people are expected to attend the dedication ceremony of our new MacArthur Lock tomorrow afternoon.

They have a right to know that there have been rumors of an attack on the locks during the ceremony that seem to have come from inside the Nazi Party itself.

Whether the rumors are correct and an attack is imminent is a matter of conjecture at this point.

On the plus side is that if the attack should come we'll be ready for it. Barrage balloons will thwart an air attack and torpedo nets will guard from attacks from underwater. The military is on full-alert and soldiers are manning an arsenal of anti-aircraft weapons.

On the minus side is that we have no solid information on an attack and where it might come from. U.S. officials have feared the Nazis might bring in planes piece by piece by U-boat and assemble them in the Canadian north woods. Such an operation would have to include a significant airstrip and would be readily visible from the air. So far U.S. and Canadian forces have failed to find any sign of an airstrip or any buildings where planes might be assembled.

Tomorrow Governor Kelly and Senator Vandenberg will join hundreds of officials, military personnel and private citizens in dedicating the newest Soo lock.

They know well of the possibilities of a Nazi attack. They will be on hand, and so will I.

Whether you choose to join us is up to you. But at least you are now aware of the possible danger.

87

Pam's Coffee Shop was so packed with people that Andy and I were forced to squeeze into two stools against the window facing out onto Portage. The locks were just across the way.

We sat side by side, our coffee cups resting on a shelf that ran the length of the window. Andy was dressed in a well-worn pair of blue jeans; he had instructed me to wear old slacks and bring along a light jacket. With the temperature predicted to approach seventy-five degrees today I wondered why.

I sipped my coffee, black. I decided against enjoying a cigarette along with it, the place was too crowded and already filled with smoke.

"I stopped by the office this morning, early," Andy said. "Wire service says our troops are invading southern Sicily as we speak. Patton and Monty are leading the charge."

I nodded. "They've been softening up the area with bombing raids for the last couple of days."

"G.P.'s editorial ran this morning, warning people about the possibility of a Nazi bombing raid attack during the ceremony. What kind of odds are you giving on an attack?"

The sixty-four dollar question. "Your guess is as good as mine," I said. "But the authorities are sure taking the chances seriously."

"My dad calls it hogwash," Andy said. "My mom's scared though." I had forgotten that Andy still lived with his parents.

Andy paused looking down at his coffee mug, then back up at me. "You really think Shirley Benoit found out something about the raid? And that she was murdered by a German agent?"

"Why would you ask me that, Andy? I never said anything more about Shirley than that she was my best friend."

Andy blushed. "You're right. But you must have known. I overheard your uncle and Crawford talking about Shirley being with the FBI."

"What else did you hear, Andy?"

"Not much. They shooed me away when they saw me at the door."

"I see." I decided to trust Andy with what I had learned about Shirley's background from the Bergmans.

Andy shook his head when I'd finished. "It's all so surreal," he said. "I grew up in the Soo. It's a small town. We're not used to having FBI agents posing as waitresses, or . . . or gangsters walking the streets. We're not used to someone being murdered every other day. Who's behind all this, anyway?"

This time I shook my head. "I wish I knew."

"I couldn't go to war, but now the war's coming home to me. The way things are going, nothing would surprise me. What's next, your uncle being arrested as a Nazi spy?"

"I think that's one thing we *don't* have to worry about," I said.

"I'm not so sure about Crawford, though," Andy said.

"Jack Crawford? What do you mean?"

Andy seemed to struggle with the words. "I don't think he's who he says he is, that's all. I've thought from the beginning that he doesn't know beans about editing a newspaper."

Andy's thoughts echoed my own, but my uncle's words rang in my head: *Do you think I'd hire anyone who wouldn't be good for the paper?*

"What makes you doubt Crawford's credentials?" I asked.

"Just some little things," Andy said. "Like when Crawford first got here in January, he didn't know what a paste up room was."

"Did you ask him about that?"

"Sure, but he made up a story. Said they called it the makeup room in Cleveland."

"Maybe they did."

"Yeah, but there were other things," Andy said.

"Why didn't you say something to someone? Like my uncle?"

Andy hesitated. "You have to understand. I've wanted to be a reporter since I was in high school. Mr. Crawford always encouraged me. I didn't dare to risk everything by criticizing him. Besides, they were all small things. Taken one at a time, they wouldn't have proven anything."

"I do find his judgment troubling," I admitted. "The way he refused to let me phone my sources in Detroit to write a firsthand account of the rioting. Said we had enough from the wire services.

"But while we're confiding in each other, Andy, I have a question."

"Shoot."

"Why did you insist that I dress this way, in a pair of slacks I'd almost thrown away? And what's so special about this coffee shop?"

He stood up and drained his mug. "C'mon. I'll show you."

88

"Here we are," Andy said.

We were standing at the intersection of West Portage and Magazine streets, a short walk from Pam's Coffee Shop and across the street from the grassy park that separated the street from the locks. A ten-foot high chain-link fence guarded the park and locks beyond it.

"Here? Why are we here?" We were in the middle of the street. I didn't get it.

Andy reached down and, after some grunting and groaning, picked up what looked like a manhole cover. It rolled away with some effort and we both looked down into a dark hole.

"You know all about gathering background for a news story, right?"

"Of course."

Andy smiled. "We're going to gather *under* ground."

"What are you talking about?" I glanced around and all I could see was the huge chain-link fence between us and the locks.

"Don't worry about the fence," Andy said. "We'll be walking underneath the park."

"Underneath?"

"Yeah, we're going to see the new MacArthur Lock from below."

Andy was already climbing down into the hole, going hand over hand on the metal rungs that had been positioned into the concrete wall of the tunnel. I followed closely, glad that Andy had told me to wear slacks.

I stepped down onto the cement floor in a small pool of light that came from above. It felt cool away from the sunlight and I pulled the light jacket around me. Andy switched his flashlight on and I could see damp cement walls that faded into darkness ahead. As we began to walk into the darkness, our footsteps echoed against the walls. The air was damp and smelled of mildew.

"How did you find this tunnel?" I asked.

"One of the soldiers from the Army Corps of Engineers tipped me off," Andy said. "The tunnels run underneath the locks carrying hydraulic and electrical lines. They're also used for locks maintenance."

As we walked, following the beam from the flashlight Andy held, I felt thankful I didn't suffer from claustrophobia. I'd be running for the exit if I did. The damp cement walls seemed to close in on either side, although I'm sure it was my imagination playing tricks.

Andy must have read my mind. "The walls get a little narrower here but they'll widen out as we get near the locks," he said.

We were getting close, I reasoned, because the space between the walls now was widening. Suddenly we were inside a dark, cement-walled room. As Andy shined his light against the far wall, I could see huge gears that made the space look like the inside of a giant watch.

"This is as far as we go," Andy announced. We stopped and examined the workings of the new MacArthur Lock from thirty feet or so underneath. "On the other side of that wall is the lock," Andy said. He pointed to the gears. "Those are what cause the gates of the Lock to open and close."

Just then a deafening roar sounded, and I nearly jumped out of my skin. The gears began to rotate.

"Relax," Andy said. "They're just testing the gates."

"Where does that ladder go?" I asked, pointing to a series of metal rungs climbing up the wall to a trap door similar to the one we had entered.

"It opens out onto the MacArthur Lock," Andy said. "I climbed up the other day and surprised the hell out of an Army private who happened to be on guard. I had to talk fast to convince him I was on official newspaper business. I told him I had simply stumbled across the opening to the tunnel out on Portage Street and was just trying to see where it led."

"And he believed you?"

"Well, I'm not in the brig. C'mon, let's go back and check out the new lock from above."

89

Claus Krueger watched the two reporters emerge from the tunnel from a distance of two hundred meters.

A safe distance; they would never see him. Now, as they came closer, walking toward the public entrance to the locks, he ducked into Adams' Hardware.

He was on Portage Avenue for a last minute examination of the grounds around the locks. He made mental notes of the location of the hundred or so folding chairs set up almost to the edge of the new lock. He made note of where the bulk of the crowd would stand behind them.

There would be at least two thousand visitors here tomorrow. The more the merrier.

How had Roosevelt put it? December 7, 1941 - a date that would live in infamy?

July 11, 1943, was going to top that.

90

Andy and I had been tapped to write an article profiling some of the workers of the Great Lakes Dredge and Dock Company for tomorrow's special dedication edition. These fellows had worked fourteen months straight in shifts that ran around the clock, in freezing cold and blistering heat, and they had built the MacArthur Lock in sixteen months. Years ago, the Weizel and Poe Locks had taken eight years to complete and the Davis Lock took six.

As we got to the gate, security was tight. An Army M.P. checked our credentials carefully as we entered the fenced area. The MacArthur Lock was closest to land, and a hundred or so folding chairs had been set up on the grass at the edge of the lock for tomorrow's ceremony. The chairs were earmarked for the ceremony participants, their families and guests. Regular folks who got here early would take up the back rows, and there was a large area behind the chairs where visitors would stand. It was clear officials expected a large crowd in spite of G.P.'s editorial.

Andy and I split up. I interviewed half a dozen workers and then took a last look around the area. To my left, out toward the end of the MacArthur Lock, where it flowed into the St. Marys River, I spotted Corporal Cummins and his sidekick with their anti-aircraft gun. Cummins waved as I approached.

"Good afternoon, Miss Brennan. Collecting background for an article?"

"Yep. Any new word from Fort Brady on an attack?"

"Nothing. But we've been on full alert since yesterday." He pointed to the ammunition clip hanging from the gun, "Old Betsy here is loaded and ready for anything the Krauts can fly at her."

"I hope you're right," I said.

The telephones were ringing when I got to the office. As I suspected, the commotion was due to G.P.'s editorial. The first call had come from our illustrious mayor Roland Swenson, but others followed. The pressure on G.P. had been tremendous.

Not all the calls were negative; some praised G.P. for having the guts to run the editorial. Some callers merely had questions.

News of the war continued to pour in from the wire services all afternoon: an armada of some 2,700 ships was approaching the island of Sicily from virtually every port on the Mediterranean.

I was home soon after five, let Mick out and fixed supper for myself.

I was in bed by eleven. Tomorrow was the Big Day.

But I could never have guessed just how big it would be.

91

July 11, 1943
D-Day

Early on the day of the dedication, Andy Checkle and I stood beside the St. Marys River at the site of the original Fort Brady. Built in 1822, it was now a city park. Scotty had sailed the Caiman up here, just half a mile or so east of the locks. The huge yacht was moored at the dock just feet from us, ready to sail into the MacArthur Lock later in the day.

The sun shone bright and the temperature felt hot even at ten o'clock in the morning. The day promised to be a scorcher.

A crowd had gathered in the park to get a look at the ship they'd been reading about in the newspapers. Suddenly I heard someone call my name and turned to see Ellen Landon, my old high school chum, standing in the crowd.

We embraced, and she introduced her husband. "It's Ellen McKenzie now," she said. We spent a few moments catching up on each other's lives since graduation; then began reminiscing about our high school days. Ellen had, of course, heard about Shirley's passing.

"It was a real shocker," she said. "It seems like yesterday we all met at Toad Hall, talking about teachers and . . ." her face reddened as she glanced at her husband, "boyfriends." We both laughed as she told her husband, "That was before I met you, Honey."

But Ellen's comments about our Toad Hall hit me like a thunderbolt. Suddenly I had to find Scotty.

Andy and I bid a quick goodbye to Ellen and her husband and ran aboard the Caiman.

We found Scotty guiding a vacuum over the carpeted floor of the main salon.

"Scotty, I think I know where Shirley's diary is," I called over the roar of the vacuum.

Scotty turned off the vacuum; I had his attention. He listened as I told him about Toad Hall and why I thought the odds were good that Shirley had hidden her diary there.

"So you see, we've got to get to the Minneapolis Woods for a look around right away."

Scotty seemed skeptical. "How can you be certain this Toad Hall of yours is still there?" he asked.

"I can't," I said. "But it's our last chance to find the notes Shirley kept during her investigation. It's sure worth a try."

"People will be arriving to board the Caiman in less than two hours," Scotty said. "Can't it wait until after the ceremony?"

"Don't you see? It may be too late after the ceremony. If there's an attack, people will be dead. I need you to go with me. Andy can drive to town and file our story with the paper."

"There's too much for me to do here," Scotty said. "Stay and help, then I'll drive you there as soon as the dedication is over."

"I'm going now," I said. "Either you go with me, or I'll get Andy to drive me."

"What about your story?"

"Hell with the story. I'm talking about people's lives. Maybe hundreds or thousands of them."

Scotty drew a deep sigh. "Alright. I'll go with you. But I damn well hope this isn't some wild goose chase."

Andy drove us the eight miles downriver to Scotty's Packard, then turned around and headed for the newspaper.

The dedication loomed just hours away.

92

Scotty's Packard made good time. We reached the Minneapolis Woods in fifteen minutes.

We left the Packard beside the road in front of the old Frederick's mansion, a colonial style house that had seen better days. Much better. Windows were broken, the roof had caved in on one side and weeds replaced what had once been an elegant lawn. We walked around to the back of the house and after searching for a minute or two found the trail that led back toward Toad Hall.

Plant life had encroached on much of the trail making it narrower than I remembered. We followed the path as it wound around a gigantic oak and down a slight hill. We walked until we could see the cabin up ahead. It, too, had been a victim of overly aggressive plant life. As we came closer, though, I could see that brush had been cleared from around the doorway, making it possible to enter and leave.

Someone had been at Toad Hall within the past few weeks.

The old door creaked as we entered the cabin, stepping from the warmth of a July day into a cool, damp and somewhat bleak interior. I looked around the living room, streams of light coming in through windows that had long ago given up their glass. A table sat in the center of the room, wooden chairs were scattered about, some lying on their sides. Toward the rear there were two bedrooms and a bathroom. To the left sat a giant stone fireplace that hadn't felt the heat of a fire in three decades.

The smell of the cabin interior was exactly as I remembered: a musty combination of wood and plants. The whole scene was pure nostalgia. As I gazed about the room I could picture the five of us. Shirley, Sue, Mary, Ellen and me sitting around this very table, telling stories and laughing uproariously.

That seemed so very long ago now.

It was time to get to work. The main room took seconds to search; there was nowhere to store anything. I headed for one of the bedrooms and hit pay dirt almost immediately.

93

Andy Checkle reached the *News* office just after noon. The parking lot adjacent to the *Soo Morning News* was filled with employees' cars, so he drove two storefronts farther and parked in the city lot.

He sprinted to the office, anxious to file the story of the Caiman preparations and meet Kate back at the locks for the dedication ceremony. That was the real story today, and the *News* had promised a special edition to hit the stands later this evening.

Once inside the building, Checkle hurried to his desk. He spread his notes on the desk and began typing almost immediately. The story seemed to go as smoothly as the preparations aboard the Caiman.

When he finished fifteen minutes later, he looked up and noticed something was wrong. Mary Nelson was dabbing her eyes with a handkerchief.

He approached her desk. "Something wrong, Mary?"

She looked up. "You haven't heard?"

"Heard what?"

"G.P. He's in the hospital. He had a heart attack."

The shock ran down to his toes. "A heart attack? How bad? How is he?"

"No one seems to know," Nelson said. Her voice broke as she said, "Why, we're all in the dark."

As Checkle looked around, he noticed for the first time the worried expressions on the faces of his co-workers.

The pressure had finally gotten to G.P. The man who nothing seemed to faze had succumbed after all. Checkle knew he had to get to Kate with the news. But he needed to know more. How serious was the attack? Was

G.P. conscious? Kate would ask questions about her uncle's condition and she deserved more than, "we're all in the dark."

He ran for his car and set off for the hospital.

94

Entering the bedroom, I immediately noticed a single bed that sat against the far wall of the room. The bed was simple enough, a wooden frame and a slightly rusted bedspring covered by an old mattress. I approached it and when I lifted the mattress my heart skipped a beat. On top of the bedsprings lay a writing tablet. The kind kids use in school.

"Scotty, come in here." I picked up the tablet and let the mattress fall back into place. As I opened the cover and glanced at the first page I recognized Shirley's handwriting immediately.

I looked up to see Scotty in the doorway. "Shirley kept a journal," I said. "This had to be what the person who searched her house was after."

"Give it to me, Kate."

I leafed through the journal. "Look, Scotty. Shirley wrote entries on a daily basis. Starting in January when she came back to the Soo."

"Let me have the journal." Scotty was now standing next to me. His voice sounded strange, demanding and nervous all at the same time. Ignoring him, I continued skimming the pages. I found notations concerning shipments of dynamite and other explosives to the Banyon Mining Company in Sault Ste. Marie.

"Kate. Give . . . the . . . tablet . . . to . . . me."

"What's in here that you don't want me to see?"

"Just hand it over and we'll forget all about it." He grabbed for the notebook and we wrestled for a moment. He finally tore it out of my hand.

"Scotty, Shirley was working for the FBI. Why don't you want me to read what she wrote?"

Before he could answer, a newspaper clipping fell from the tablet. I leaned over and picked it up.

As I read the headline, and the story underneath the picture of a young, blond-haired man, the entire room seemed to grow cold.

95

Banyon Copper Mining Heir Dies in Fiery Auto Crash

Phoenix, Arizona, July 3, 1934 – The son of the late copper scion Martin Banyon of Iron Mountain died in the wreck of his Duesenberg convertible coupe outside Phoenix on Tuesday night.

Witnesses say Martin "Scotty" Banyon, 22, had been racing a black Chevrolet convertible when he failed to negotiate a sharp curve along a highway north of Phoenix and his car rolled over several times before coming to a stop at the bottom of a steep hill.

Coroner Edward Littleton said Banyon died instantly. There were no passengers in the car.

Banyon had been the sole surviving member of the Banyon family that had moved to Phoenix from Iron Mountain 10 years ago. Martin Banyon Sr., the founder and former CEO of Banyon Copper Mining Enterprises, suffered a fatal heart attack in Phoenix in 1924, shortly after the move. His wife, Beatrice, died a year later.

Funeral arrangements are incomplete.

96

I looked up at the man who stood in front of me. The man I thought I knew, but hadn't known at all.

"Who are you?" I asked.

He took a deep breath and his reply sent shivers through me.

"My name is Claus Krueger."

My heart and my brain were pulled in opposite directions as I realized there was little doubt that I was looking at the killer of my best friend.

"You're a Nazi. You murdered Shirley Benoit."

He hesitated. "Yes."

"She was a defenseless woman. A woman with everything to live for. How could you kill someone like that?"

His lips pursed. "I'm a soldier, Kate. Your country and mine are at war."

"You're not a soldier. You're a damned assassin . . . a spy."

"I am a soldier. And a soldier follows orders."

"Your orders were to kill an innocent woman?"

"My orders were and are to deal with anyone who gets in the way. Your friend came close to discovering the details of my mission."

"Then you'd better kill me, because I intend to get in your way anyway I can."

He grabbed my wrists and held them together with terrible force.

I said, "If you're going to kill me, do it and get it over with."

"I'm not going to kill you, Kate."

He was holding my hands so tightly that struggling seemed impossible. He dragged me from the bedroom out into the main room of the cottage.

"Why be so kind to me? Why not murder me, too?"

He picked up one of the old wooden chairs that had been lying sideways on the floor and pushed me down into it.

"I could have killed you easily when I followed you to Negaunee. Or I could have let that mob gunman do the job instead of killing him.

"There's no need to kill you when I can make certain you can't warn anyone in time to do anything about it. Afterwards, I'll call the Morning News office and tell them where to find you."

He reached into his pocket and pulled out a small roll of some kind of masking tape. He bent down and taped one of my arms and then the other, to the arms of the chair.

"Your own military invented this tape," Scotty said. "They're calling it one-hundred-mile-per-hour tape because it holds tight even in hurricane-force winds."

The bonds felt uncomfortable, but the pain seemed bearable.

"So G.P.'s information was right. There is going to be an attack."

"Yes. And the only way your government could have learned of it is that the Enigma Code must have been compromised. That information will be invaluable to the Third Reich."

"And what's your part in this? Directing German dive bombers to the locks?"

Scotty smiled. "There are no bombers, Kate. Even our best dive bombers couldn't penetrate the defenses your army has in place."

"What then?"

"The explosion that destroys your locks will be as unexpected as it is deadly.

"It will come from below and within."

97

"What the hell are you talking about?"

Scotty was taping my right leg to the leg of the chair. He moved to the other side of the chair and taped my leg to the chair leg there.

Satisfied I couldn't move, he stood in front of me. He set the rest of the roll of tape on the table.

"I've been receiving shipments of dynamite," he said. "Tons of it. Miners use explosives to open mineshafts. It was easy for me, as Scotty Banyon, to receive hundreds of pounds at a time."

He smiled. "Dynamite is scarce with the war on. I couldn't have done it without the help of your government."

"So you're going to dynamite the locks? Fat chance. You can't get near them."

"I already have. My men acted last night. The tunnel beneath the locks is packed with explosives. There's more aboard the Caiman. Her hold is full of it. Once we've sailed into the MacArthur Lock, I'll set a timer, which will ignite the explosives in the Caiman's hold. The concussion will cause the dynamite under the locks to blow."

"You'll kill thousands of innocent civilians at the dedication ceremony."

"We're at war, Kate. People die in wars."

"But women and children? What kind of government gives an order like that?"

"You have to understand, Kate. There were thousands of innocent women and children killed in Germany during the Great War, as Americans like to call it. To German people, there was nothing great about it. The war and the Treaty of Versailles afterwards left Germany helpless."

Scotty turned toward the door.

"Your Hitler started the war," I called.

He whirled back to face me. "And this time we're going to finish it. The Fuhrer will stop at nothing short of total victory."

"Your Fuhrer is a mad man."

"A mad man who single handedly pulled Germany out of economic ruin and restored pride to its citizens."

"And now wants to kill American civilians."

"No different from the way your soldiers killed German citizens in the last war. Americans think they are untouchable because they can hide between two oceans."

He started toward the door again. "Today, they'll learn the foolishness of that thinking."

I called to him. "Wait!"

He stopped and turned back to me. "Yes? What is it?"

"You were obviously planning to kill me, too. I would have been aboard the Caiman."

"No. You would have been detained by the two men who work for me. They had orders to kidnap you and hold you hostage at the building where I stored the explosives. You would have been released shortly after the locks were demolished."

"I'll tell the sheriff and the Army everything I know."

"They won't find me. My return home to Germany is already arranged. I'll disappear during the chaos that follows the explosion. A submarine is scheduled to pick me up off the Canadian shore in two days."

"Why tell me that if you're going to let me live?"

"The Canadian shoreline runs for thousands of miles. Without knowing exactly where the rendezvous point is, your ships will never find me."

"Why spare me?"

Scotty walked back to me, stopping just short of my chair. He paused for a moment before he spoke, his face looked strangely sad. "Kate, I've done something no soldier should do. I've become infatuated with you.

"What happens today will almost certainly guarantee a German victory. The war will end soon and afterwards I plan to come back to America and find you. Maybe . . . maybe with the situation completely different, we might make a life together."

"Don't count on it."

He turned and walked out the door, leaving me alone to contemplate the horror that would take place in less than two hours.

98

Andy Checkle was aware that the victim of a recent heart attack wouldn't be allowed visitors and was prepared to flash his press card and claim official business. But the hospital receptionist was on the telephone when he entered the lobby. Ignoring her frantic waves, he ran for the stairwell.

He took steps two at a time on the way to the third floor. Once there he followed the arrows to the ICU which consisted of two large rooms, one for men, the other for women. Entering the men's ward, he found a pale, wan-appearing G.P. lying in one of the three beds.

He approached the bed and placed a tentative hand on G.P.'s exposed thin white arm. The old man's eyes opened slowly.

"What the hell are you doing here?" G.P.'s words were strong, his voice weak. "There's a story to cover."

"Sorry, Mr. Brennan. I heard you . . . you were sick. Kate doesn't know, yet. I wanted to tell her . . . that I saw you."

"Where is Kate?"

"She's with Scotty Banyon."

"At the dedication?" G.P. struggled to sit up, but fell back onto the pillow.

"That's not 'til later, Mr. Brennan. Kate thinks she remembered where her friend Shirley might have left records ... a diary she might have kept during her investigation. Kate says Shirley worked for the FBI."

The old man's eyes shut tight, then opened again. "She did," he said.

"You knew?"

"Yes. She was killed . . ." his voice trailed off. It seemed like he might fall asleep, but his eyes opened again. "Checkle . . . Jack Crawford is going to need your help. Yours and Kate's."

"How so, Mr. Brennan?"

"I'm going to be here awhile. I can't even get out of this damn bed without some nurse having a fit."

"Yes, sir. You need to rest."

"But Crawford needs you. You and Kate. You see . . ." The old man struggled for words. "Crawford isn't a newspaper editor. He has no experience outside of his college newspaper. I've been backing him up, and now I'm . . ."

"If he's not an editor, what is he Mr. Brennan?"

G.P. took a deep breath. "Crawford works for the government." Noticing Checkle's startled expression, he decided to begin again. "Ever heard of Darby's Rangers?"

"Who hasn't? They're commandos."

"Crawford was there when the Rangers attacked the Vichy French Fort of Batterie du Nord at Algiers last November. The raid was a resounding success, but Crawford was wounded."

"Crawford? A ranger?"

"One of the very toughest. He recovered from his wounds back in the States. He had worked for the FBI before enlisting in the Army, so the Army reassigned him here in the Soo. Undercover."

"That's why he didn't seem to know much about editing a newspaper."

G.P. nodded. "Now go tell Kate what I told you. She'll have to act as editor-in-chief today. Crawford's going to be at the locks this afternoon in case the Nazis attack."

Checkle started for the door but turned back. "I've got to tell Kate how you're doing."

"Tell her I'm going to live. Now get the hell out of here."

99

Harry Houdini died in Detroit's Grace Hospital when I was eleven years old. I loved magic, and I remembered reading at the time that Houdini's great "escapes" were predicated on keeping his hands and arms tensed while the bonds were applied. When he relaxed them afterwards, his bonds were actually loose.

I had tried the same technique when Scotty – Krueger – had taped my hands and legs to the chair. Now as I relaxed I could feel some "wiggle room" in my bonds.

Not much. But maybe enough.

Ten minutes went by. Then half-an-hour. I still struggled with the damn tape. So much for a second career as an escape artist.

I felt frustrated and angry. Sick to my stomach. Thousands of innocent people were going to die in just over an hour and I was helpless to stop it.

I was also dying for a cigarette. My purse was on the table next to me, but all I could do was look at the pack of Chesterfields.

In frustration I pulled frantically at the tape that bound my hands and feet to the wooden chair. As I rocked, the chair wobbled and I heard it creak. This old wooden chair had been at Toad Hall since we met here years ago and it was on its last legs. Literally.

Encouraged, I rocked from side to side and heard the "creaks" get louder and louder. Each time I rocked left or right, I felt the chair give way a bit more.

Ten more minutes went by. The tape held strong, but the chair was coming apart. Finally I could pull the right arm away from the rest of the chair and reach over to my left side. Bit by bit I pulled at the tape, unwrapping my left arm. Once it was free, I struggled to pull the tape from my right arm.

Once both arms were free, I bent down and unwrapped my legs, thankful I had shaved them this morning.

I stood up and walked weakly back and forth in the room, rubbing my legs until I felt the blood returning.

I lit a cigarette as I headed for the door. I needed a lift back to town. The 131st Infantry headquarters was nearby, but I knew with all the people pouring into town for the dedication, there'd be plenty of cars to choose from on Ashmun Street. As I approached the street I remembered the famous scene from *It Happened One Night*. I had seen the movie as a senior in high school and recalled how Clark Gable and Claudette Colbert were forced to hitch a ride. Gable couldn't get motorists to stop, so Colbert pulled her dress up over her knee, stuck her leg out at the side of the road and cars came screeching to a halt.

What the hell, it was worth a try.

Ashmun was as busy as I had expected. The first car was coming away from town not toward it, but I lifted my skirt and stuck my leg out anyway. I felt disappointment when it continued past. But I felt gratified when the driver screeched to a halt down the road and did a U-turn, almost sideswiping another car coming the opposite way.

That was more like it. I was congratulating myself on my feminine wiles as the car pulled up beside me.

I returned to earth when I saw Andy Checkle at the wheel.

100

As we drove toward town, Andy and I traded bits of information, each filling in our own pieces of the puzzle. A lot of questions were answered as we made our way north on Ashmun.

I told Andy about Scotty Banyon, aka Claus Krueger, and the part he was playing in an all too real attack on the locks. I told him about the dynamite planted in the tunnel he and I explored the day before and on board the Caiman.

Andy nodded as I told him that Krueger had murdered Shirley when she got too close to the truth. He had guessed as much from what I had already said.

Then it was Andy's turn to surprise me. Jack Crawford an Army Ranger? I guess Andy's suspicions had been right after all. And I would have bet a month's salary that Crawford's cover as managing editor of the *Soo Morning News* had been arranged with my uncle's help and cooperation. G.P.'s dedication to his country was well known, as he had received awards from local, state and federal governments -- and from even President Roosevelt himself -- for his support of government activities. When he spoke of his "Washington contacts" one could only guess how high up they went.

Andy wondered why anyone hadn't caught on to Claus Krueger. I explained how his masquerade as Scotty Banyon had been impeccably planned and executed. Years had passed since the real Scotty Banyon's family had moved from the western Upper Peninsula to Arizona. As the man who promised newfound wealth in the form of copper mining jobs, no one had questioned his credentials. Krueger had been welcomed into the community with open arms.

It would be a gross understatement to say that the whole situation had a profound effect on me. The way the man I knew as Scotty Banyon had toyed with my emotions was unforgivable. Maybe I could have found some solace in the fact I wasn't the only one taken in, but truthfully, it didn't help much. Did I want to strangle him? At the moment strangulation seemed much too kind a death.

Traffic on Ashmun became much heavier as we approached the downtown area. We seemed to be crawling at a maddeningly slow pace as automobiles rode bumper to bumper into the small town not used to being the center of attention. I glanced over at the crowded sidewalk and noticed pedestrians were walking faster than we could drive.

We might have gotten out of the car and walked, but there was absolutely no place to park. Every parking place was taken; every lot was filled with cars.

We finally reached Arlington Street and turned left, narrowly avoiding an oncoming car. Luckily the *Morning News* lot was being patrolled by a guard who waved us in when he recognized Andy's car. We found a space in the far corner of the lot and ran into the building.

"Mr. Crawford isn't here," Carol Olson said in her usual curt manner. "He's at the dedication of the new MacArthur Lock, of course."

Of course.

101

Considering the volume of traffic, it was faster to run the three blocks to Waters Avenue and the locks than to drive.

We arrived at the locks out of breath and sweating. The dedication was already underway. I could see soldiers standing by the half dozen anti-aircraft guns at points around the locks. They were looking skyward, not knowing the real threat came from beneath the ground.

People were seated in the hundred or so folding chairs. A couple thousand more stood to each side of the chairs and behind them. All were listening to Mayor Swenson who stood on the bow of the Caiman, now floating in the new MacArthur Lock. The Mayor was greeting the crowd and introducing the dignitaries grouped around him on the boat.

I didn't know how long we had until the entire scene would be blown into oblivion, but I knew every minute was precious.

We had to find Crawford. I shouted for Andy to start at one end of the packed visitors' area, and I'd take the other. As he ran toward the west end of the area, I began to wade into the crowd.

Army MPs were positioned the length of the lock, to make certain no one could get closer than thirty feet or so from the Caiman. I rushed up to one of them and started to explain the danger. To my immense frustration, he ignored me, keeping his eyes glued on the crowd behind me. When I tried to go around him, he blocked my way, threatening to have me arrested.

I realized I was getting nowhere. Finding Jack Crawford was next to impossible among so many people.

I earned plenty of nasty looks as I pushed through the crowd, but this wasn't a time for genteel politeness. I was here to save lives.

If I was lucky.

I finally spotted Crawford talking with an Army colonel near the stern of the Caiman, behind the line of Army MPs. Rushing up as close as I could get, I stood next to an MP and called to him. Crawford excused himself to come over to me.

"What's the trouble, Kate?"

He reacted as I expected as I explained the situation. First with disbelief, then anger.

"Where is Krueger now?" he asked.

"I have no idea," I said. "But he was going to set a charge on the explosives aboard the Caiman. He could still be there."

Crawford turned to the MP beside me. "You heard what Miss Brennan said. Help her alert the people on the Caiman and get everyone off that boat."

With that he raced toward the MacArthur Lock and the stern of the yacht.

102

As Crawford rolled over the transom onto the Caiman's teak deck, an Army MP approached carrying a rifle. Crawford reached for his wallet, flashed an identification card and the soldier saluted and backed away.

Crawford pointed to the crowd of dignitaries at the bow of the Caiman. "Get everyone off this boat," he shouted to the MP. "Now!"

The soldier, wide-eyed, ran toward the bow.

Crawford headed for the cabin door leading to the hold. Descending the steps, he found himself in a narrow hallway. Ahead lay the open door of the Caiman's large master stateroom. Hearing noises coming from inside the room, he walked quietly toward the door. He peered inside and saw the man he now knew as Claus Krueger standing next to the double bed that was covered with crates of explosive charges. Other crates ringed the bed. All were joined together with wires that led to a metal box in Krueger's hand that Crawford recognized as a timing device.

"Drop it, Krueger,"

Krueger set the timing device on the bed and smiled. "Crawford. What brings you here?"

Crawford held out his wallet with the ID card. "I'm here to see that you don't carry out your mission."

"So you're not who you appear to be either. What a coincidence. I should have known by the way you examined the corpse of the man I killed the other evening. Almost medical in your precision."

"You watched me?"

"From a few feet away. I could have broken your neck as easily as I broke his."

"You're under arrest Krueger."

"Come arrest me, Jack."

Cautiously, Crawford reached out for Krueger's shoulder to turn him around and place him in a hammerlock. Instead, Krueger grabbed Crawford's hand, threw a hip into his body and tossed him over his shoulder like a duffel bag. Crawford landed hard on the bedroom floor.

He sprang up and rushed at Krueger, who sidestepped and deftly drove an elbow into Crawford's ribs, momentarily knocking the air from his lungs.

Krueger had been well trained in the Asian art of jujitsu. Crawford had become proficient enough in jujitsu during his training as an Army Ranger, but preferred the more traditional boxing that he had practiced as a youth in the gyms of Chicago. His string of victories had culminated in the 1939 all-Army heavyweight championship.

"Come on, Crawford, what are you waiting for?"

Crawford glanced from Krueger to the timing device attached to the explosive charges. Nearly a minute had elapsed since he had interrupted the German. Up above and ashore, thousands of lives were at stake.

Krueger noticed his gaze. "You haven't much time, Crawford. The device is set for fifteen minutes, and sixty seconds have already gone by. We can play this game for the next fourteen minutes. I'm not afraid to die for my country. Are you willing to die for yours?"

Crawford circled the crouching German, praying for a clear shot with his right hand; just one, at the man's jaw. In years past he had brought down many an opponent with a single right-handed blow. He would do it again.

If he got the chance.

He feinted with the right hand and, as Krueger began to react, rocked him back with a left jab that glanced off the cheek.

Krueger shook his head violently and returned to his original crouch. "Time is growing short Crawford," he said. "You've got to come to me."

Crawford closed in, throwing a right hand that Krueger dodged and then grabbed hold of. Grasping the hand, Krueger again threw the man over his shoulder and to the floor. This time he held onto the hand tightly, then whirled until his right foot was immediately above the American's face. Crawford turned his face just in time to partially deflect the downward thrust of the foot, but the side of his head screamed with pain.

Yanking his hand from Krueger's grasp, he rolled to his right and found room to stand. Krueger, still upright, affected the classic jujitsu fighting position.

Krueger was quicker than anyone Crawford had boxed, even during the all-Army championships. But Crawford knew he was faster than anyone Krueger had ever fought.

Just one solid blow with his right hand.

Moving in closer, he feinted with a left, then with a right. Krueger went for the second feint, grasping air just in time to catch a wicked left hook to the jaw that staggered him back.

Shaking his head, he looked to his left, at the timing device. "Twelve minutes, seven seconds," he said. "Come get me Crawford."

Both men circled, Krueger crouched in the stance of the Asian martial art. Crawford feinted with a right then followed with a feint of his left hand that Krueger fell for, exposing the left side of his face.

It was the opening Crawford had been praying for. With the strength and speed of a steel trap, he sent Krueger to the floor for good with a solid right hook to the jaw.

It was the American way.

103

I was at the bow of the Caiman ushering the last of the VIPs down the gangplank when Crawford sprang up on deck shouting to open the lock gate.

He disappeared into the yacht's salon and reappeared a few seconds later at the helm twenty feet above us.

At an agonizingly slow pace, the lock's gate began to open onto the western waters of the St. Marys. I heard the Caiman's engines spring to life with a roar and the yacht began moving forward. As it did, the gangplank began to shatter and I leapt off onto the shore just in time.

The MacArthur Lock stretched 800 feet and there were still 300 feet or so to go before the Caiman would exit into the River. The lock gates had opened barely wide enough for the ship to pass as Crawford maneuvered her through and into open water.

The yacht's engines screamed at full throttle now, waves of white foam kicking up behind her as she dashed for the open water of the two-mile-wide head of the St. Marys River.

I stood at the side of the lock watching the ship become smaller and smaller. Once Crawford determined he was out far enough for the cargo to explode without igniting the huge cache of dynamite below all of us, he cut the engines.

In the silence that followed, I swear I could actually hear my heart pounding.

The Caiman had to be a mile away and I could barely see Crawford as he appeared on the ship's deck. I watched him dive into the St. Marys frigid water and begin to swim toward shore. I closed my eyes in silent prayer that he could swim clear of the area before the dynamite in the Caiman's hold exploded.

That's when I heard a sound that made the hair on the back of my neck stand at attention.

The Caiman's engines were roaring to life again.

104

Something had to be done. Fast.

As I gazed out to the point of the river where the Caiman was now becoming terrifyingly larger, my eye caught the specter of Corporal Roy Cummins and Private Joe Johnson standing at the side of Old Betsy at the end of the lock.

My heart racing, I took off my high heels and ran the four hundred feet to where they stood. I was out of breath when I reached them.

"What's happening, Miss Brennan?"

"That boat is loaded with explosives and the man piloting it is trying to get it back here. It'll destroy the locks and kill everyone."

Corporal Cummins swung the barrel of his anti-aircraft weapon toward the onrushing Caiman. "I'll blow her out of the water."

"You've had enough trouble with the authorities, Corporal. You aim the gun. I'll do the rest."

Cummins looked through the sight for a moment then turned to me. "Old Betsy is pointed directly where that boat will be in five seconds," he said. "Johnson, get ready to feed the ammunition."

I looked out into the river where the man I had once fallen in love with was about to die by my hand.

Could I do it?

Are you serious? Could I kill the man who had played my heart like a cheap guitar . . . the man who now threatened to kill thousands of my fellow Americans?

"Goodbye, Scotty."

I grabbed the handle of Old Betsy and pressed the trigger.

105

The explosion blasted the Caiman from timbers to toothpicks and its reverberations blew out store windows up and down Portage Avenue and beyond.

But fortunately the yacht was far enough off shore that the thousands of pounds of dynamite packed in the tunnel under the unsuspecting crowd never ignited.

A crew removed it, gingerly, the next day.

Jack Crawford gave me a real scare. After diving off the Caiman, he disappeared in the water and I feared he had succumbed to the blast. I breathed a huge sigh of relief when he swam ashore not far from the MacArthur Lock. I felt so glad to see him that I embarrassed myself by giving him a hug, wet as he was.

Difficult as it seems to imagine, the dedication ceremony continued after a half hour pause. In spite of the momentary excitement the crowd was blissfully unaware of how close to annihilation they had come.

Awards were presented, including the Army-Navy "E" award to the workers of the Great Lakes Dredge and Dock Company for their efforts in working around the clock to complete the MacArthur Lock in record time.

The U.S. Government took great pains to cover up the story of what really happened at Sault Ste. Marie that day, of how close America had come to a disaster that could easily have changed the course of the war. Authorities feared that Americans would be demoralized if they knew how close the Nazis had come to attacking us within our own borders.

The secret of the breaking of the top-secret Enigma code died with Scotty. The Germans never learned that the Allies knew what they were going to do before they did it. Actually, Polish experts had broken the code in 1939. They handed the secret over to the British just before their country was overrun by the Nazi blitzkrieg.

In all the commotion that day, few people had seen what actually happened. I was at the far end of the lock, away from the crowd, when I pulled the trigger on the anti-aircraft gun. They heard the explosion, of course, but the official word was that the yacht's engine had overheated and the boat had been piloted out into the river just in time.

Open a history book today and you'll read that the freighter Carl D. Bradley was the first boat to use the MacArthur Lock, and in a way it was. The Bradley had been scheduled to be the first freighter through the MacArthur and was positioned out in the river just a few hundred yards away.

The Caiman and its owner have been conveniently forgotten.

The two men who worked for Scotty were arrested. The government originally planned to try them for treason. But the men testified that while they knew they were breaking the law, they were unaware that Scotty Banyon was a German agent. They were convicted of fraud and served ten-year sentences.

G.P. was released from the hospital after a three-week stay. He recuperated at home, but returned to the *Morning News* long before the doctors had recommended. He was a tough old bird, tougher even than a heart attack.

It took me longer to recover. My wounds ran deeper than even I had imagined. After a year of grieving the loss of Ronny, I had healed enough to think I was in love with another man. Now that he had died by my own hand, I found myself empty of emotion for months afterward. I consoled myself writing the story of Shirley's role with the FBI and why she died. Like all of those who serve their country during this and other critical times, she was a true American hero.

I eventually returned to the *Detroit Times* to continue my investigative reporting of the mob's counterfeiting of rationing stamps.

Andy Checkle turned into a first rate reporter, moving on to Chicago and winning the Pulitzer Prize for his stories about that city's battle with corruption in local government.

Corporal Roy Cummins attained the rank of sergeant before being honorably discharged at war's end and returning to Louisiana Negro

Normal and Industrial Institute where he helped Coach Eddie Robinson establish the school as a major football power. Louisiana Negro Normal became Grambling College in 1946. Roy Cummins was a leader in the Civil Rights Movement of the 1960s.

Felice Miller eventually married a doctor from the Canadian Sault Ste. Marie across the river and had four children.

How had Jack Crawford managed to trick everyone at the *Morning News* into believing he was an honest-to-goodness newspaper editor? I'd like to think I wasn't fooled, but of course, I was; just like everyone else. I doubted his judgment several times, but never added two and two together and come up with four.

It seems Crawford had worked for his college newspaper and picked up enough skill to talk a decent game. And, of course, G.P. was in on the charade all along and covered for him if he made any glaring errors.

By the way, it seems Mick had Crawford figured right all along. He turned out to be a pretty decent guy.

But that's another story for another time.

Epilogue

Light from a full moon bounced across dark waters and illuminated the conning tower of German submarine U-571 that had poked its way to the surface and now lay floating approximately three hundred meters off the sandy New Brunswick coastline.

The U-boat had traveled across the North Atlantic to reach the eastern shore of Canada. It had navigated, submerged, through the Cabot Strait into the Gulf of St. Lawrence last evening.

Two men stood on deck surveying the scene, one holding a pair of powerful Zeiss binoculars. The stillness of the warm summer morning was broken by the sound of waves licking the sides of the submarine.

"It will be light soon." The speaker, the older of the two, wore the uniform of a Kapitänleutnant in the German Navy. As if to punctuate his words, the first morning cries of a Piping Plover echoed across the water.

"He should be here soon," said the younger officer, glancing at his watch. "If he is coming."

"We will give him the window of time in our orders," said the Kapitänleutnant, "but no more."

"In that case, he has exactly fifteen minutes." The younger man held out a pack of Sondermischung Typ. 4. "Cigarette?"

The Kapitänleutnant took the offered cigarette and lit it, carefully cupping his hands to cover any light that might be seen from the shore. He inhaled deeply and blew out a stream of smoke. "We are precisely where we should be," he said, pointing toward the shoreline. "The small fishing village of Shippagan lies exactly three kilometers to the west. If we fail to connect, it is his fault, not ours."

Seven minutes passed. Then another seven. The morning was getting brighter. The younger man looked nervously at his watch.

"We have heard no report of the locks at Sault Ste. Marie being destroyed," he said. "Perhaps our man failed and is embarrassed to return."

The Kapitänleutnant nodded. "Or perhaps he was caught or killed." He lifted the Zeiss binoculars to his eyes for a last look at the shoreline, then turned for the hatch and motioned for the younger officer to follow.

The hatch closed and in moments the U-571 slipped silently beneath the waves and began its voyage back to the Fatherland.

© Black Rose Writing

CPSIA information can be obtained at www.ICGtesting.com
Printed in the USA
LVOW081958140113

315673LV00001B/110/P